Plain Old

KIRBY CARSON

by

Ryan ONeil

Published by:
Auriferous Books in association with Literary Underground

First Edition, 2011

Published in the United States of America

10 9 8 7 6 5 4 3 2 1

ISBN: **978-0615460260**

LITERARY
UNDERGROUND

For Lena & Andrew

Never be afraid to be YOU

Daddy Loves You :)

Thank you to my wife, Linette, and my two amazing children, Andrew and Lena; on a daily basis you let me chase my dreams and never stand in the way.

Mom, thank you for reading to me as a very young child and encouraging me to write as an adult. Thank you for all of the hard work that you put into making Kirby presentable to the public. It means more to me than you will ever know.

Steven Novak, your artistic ability is simply amazing. I thank you for your encouragement, for sharing your talent, and for your virtual friendship (we shall actually meet in person someday).

Thank you to all my friends at Literary Underground. You're all amazing in your own special way! A special thank you to MJ Heiser for your last minute helping hand.

Most of all I want to thank all of my friends who have traveled this road with me. We started out several years ago with a few simple blog posts that have since morphed into what you hold in your hands today. It means so much to me that we have experienced this journey together. Your constant and unwavering support is the fuel that feeds my engines. I could never thank you enough for that.

Lastly, thank you, Bacon.

Eminent Changes

Let's face it school was school. Sure you were there to learn, but it was also a social exercise. From your first day of nursery school to your last day of college you majored in socialization with a minor in education. It's just the way it worked.

In elementary school, you were lumped together with basically the same 30 classmates for the first six years of your educational career. You got comfortable being around these people. Some of them came and went, but the faces generally stayed the same. You became friends with some of them and tolerated the others. You knew their ins and outs. You knew instantly by looking at them if they were having a good day or a horrible day. You knew if they were really sick or if they were faking it.

All of that changed when you got to seventh grade. Your first day of middle school was like being let loose in a sprawling human zoo where hundreds of strange faces lurked around every corner. Some of those faces were happy and smiled confidently while others were almost sinister, sneering and growling as they stormed their way through the hallways leaving a wake of attitude in their path. However, most students were simply doe-eyed and confused as they scampered along looking for their next class or simply a corner in which to curl up and disappear.

It was the eighth graders who reigned supreme in middle school. They were the trendsetters and the captains of the sports teams. They were on the committees that picked the themes for the school dances and they occupied the school's elected positions such as the class President, Vice-President, Secretary, and Treasurer. They walked the hallways with a certain air of predominance that wafted around them. They were also the same students who could make life as a lowly seventh grader pure torture. Whether it was singling the seventh graders out as targets while playing dodge ball in Gym class or by playing practical jokes on them as they walked down the hallways; as a seventh grader you always had to be on your toes and expect the unexpected--when you least expected it.

The best part of being a seventh grader was when the school year ended. It was then that you knew that when summer break was completed and you returned in the fall that you would be an eighth grader. That's when it would be your turn to rule the school! You would be the one to run for class President or to be the feared bully who would play practical jokes on everyone. You would get to pick the theme for the dance where you might just get your first kiss.

However, what if just maybe you were still the same old you from last year? What if summer after summer passed and the only change that you experienced was changing your socks and underwear? What if each day you did your best to blend into the background as you attended class, as you ate lunch, and as you handed in your homework? Would that be so bad?

Right or wrong, good or bad; that's exactly what Kirby Carson did.

The Jacket

Kirby Carson transferred to Brook Harbor Elementary School sometime in the third grade. He was the kid that everyone knew of, but no one really knew much about him. The other students recognized him when they passed him in the hallway as that kid from their science class or the kid who had a locker near theirs, but you never heard of anyone getting invited to his birthday party or hanging out with him anywhere after school. It was sort of like the way that they knew their mailman; they recognized him when he was putting cards and letters into their mailbox, but they didn't know if he had a family, who his favorite football team was, or what type of music that he liked. They simply knew that he existed and it pretty much stopped there.

Kirby was sort of a loner; whether he actively wanted to be or not, he was a loner. He wasn't athletic, he wasn't a bully, he wasn't the class clown, and he surely wasn't popular. In the eyes of his fellow students, Kirby wasn't anything. He was just plain old Kirby Carson.

Even now as an eighth grader attending George Knipfing Middle School Kirby hadn't changed much at all. He was still the kid that sat in the back of the class and spoke up only when the teacher asked him a direct question. His looks hadn't changed much either. In eighth grade when everyone else was testing the waters of young adulthood and wearing new fashions or trying out makeup for the first time, Kirby had maintained his same old look that seemingly helped him to blend into the scenery. He had no apparent initiative for any sort of change at all. His hair, brown and stringy, hung over his ears on both sides and almost covered his eyes in the front. His average build allowed him to fit into the same tattered jean jacket that he had been wearing since the sixth grade; the blue denim jacket with the frayed cuffs and the large Led Zeppelin patch that covered the entire back panel. No matter what the weather was like outside, Kirby Carson could be counted on to be wearing that jean jacket. It was as if he never took it off. Some of the other students even joked that he also slept with his jacket on.

The jean jacket was one of the few Christmas gifts that he'd ever received from his father. Kirby's father had walked out when Kirby was only one year old. Kirby rarely saw him and knew very little about him. On a blustery night in the middle of Kirby's sixth grade Christmas vacation his father had flown into town and surprised Kirby and his Mom with an unannounced visit. His mother had reluctantly let him in. He stomped the snow from his shoes and walked into the apartment carrying a single package wrapped in brown paper bags and held together with duct tape.

"This is for you," said Kirby's dad when he handed him the shabbily wrapped gift.

Kirby looked up at his mom before he took the box and she nodded in approval. Kirby tore into the gift and pulled out the denim jacket. It smelled badly of stale cigarettes and wet dog.

"Go ahead. Try it on," urged his father.

Kirby had slowly put his arms through the jacket and pulled it onto his body. The overall length was a little long, but not too bad. Kirby pulled at the collar until he felt that it looked just right on him.

"Fits pretty good there Slugger!" His father had said. "Anyhow, I hate to cut this short, but my flight leaves in two hours. I'm headed off to the Caribbean and away from this snow. Gonna hit the beaches and the casinos," he laughed and nudged Kirby.

Kirby looked up at his dad and muttered, "Thanks, Dad. It was very nice of you to—"

"Well, I've got to run," interrupted his Dad. "Time's a wastin'."

As quickly as he had arrived he was gone. That was the last time that Kirby had heard from or seen his dad.

It took three washings to get the smell out before Kirby could wear the jacket without gagging. Surprisingly, and much to the dismay of his mother, Kirby actually liked the jacket once it was odorless. In early January he'd taken some of his Christmas money and bought a large patch of his favorite band, Led Zeppelin. His mom had carefully sewn the patch to the back of the jacket.

The jacket soon became an everyday part of Kirby Carson; a constant companion of sorts. His jacket was always within easy reach and he wore it wherever he went.

Project Partners

There were 26 students in Mr. Walton's American History class. Each one fidgeted in their seat as they waited anxiously to be assigned a project partner. The project would be a big part of their final grade so having just the right partner could make the difference between a passing grade and failure. Mr. Walton was also their homeroom teacher. Most of the students seemed to like him because he didn't assign too much homework and understood it when they messed up. If you accidentally showed up late for class he would joke with you about why you were late, but would rarely send anyone down to the Principal's office for punishment.

To coincide with the upcoming school elections, Mr. Walton was about to pair up the students and assign them an American President from the past that they were to write a report about and then present that report to the class at a later date. He said that he was going to randomly assign partners, but it appeared to be all too coincidental when Monika Randolph got paired with Janie Sinclair.

Monika was one of the most popular girls in the eighth grade. Most of the boys found her to be very attractive with her blond hair and the curves that she was beginning to acquire. She came from a rich family and had no problem bragging about her new bracelet or the depth of her well-stocked wardrobe. Whether the other students liked her or hated her, they all knew her.

Janie Sinclair was one of Monika's closest acquaintances and dearest admirers. While Janie didn't come from a rich family or have an expansive wardrobe she did yearn to be just like Monika in every way. Usually, wherever Monika was Janie could be found following two steps behind agreeing with whatever Monika had said.

"Sue Andrews," said Mr. Walton. "Let's see, you'll be partnered with," He paused slightly, "with Kirby Carson. Your president to research is Thomas Jefferson. Kirby? Sue? You got that?"

Kirby nodded his head quietly in acknowledgment.

"Yes, Mr. Walton," said Sue. She had a big fake grin on her face. She liked Mr. Walton and did not want to show her displeasure at being paired up with the dorkiest kid in the school. From behind her she heard the giggles and laughter of her friends as they found great amusement in her new found situation.

"Okay class," said Mr. Walton. "You are to research your president and write a ten to twelve page report about him." Sue felt a slight tap at her side, but did her best to ignore it. A few seconds later she again felt the tapping at her side and looked back and to her right. Janie was bent down tying her shoelace and attempting to pass Sue a small folded piece of paper. Sue grabbed the paper quickly while Mr. Walton wasn't looking and hid it behind her propped up history book. Slowly she opened the note trying to be as quiet as possible. Once she had the note completely unfolded she looked down at her desk to read it.

Do U heart Kirby? R U going 2 marry him and have little jean jacket wearing babies? LOL!

Kisses,

M

Sue felt Monika looking at her from behind. She quickly looked back and mouthed the words 'Ha Ha' to Monika. Monika simply grinned back at her and laughed to herself.

RINNNNNNGGGG!

"Okay class, that's all for today," said Mr. Walton as the school bell sounded the end of class.

Hurriedly, the students began to pack up their books and binders and headed for the door. Sue picked up her backpack, slung it over her shoulder, and walked out into the hallway. The halls were a hustle and bustle of activity. Everywhere you looked there were students, some of them were at their lockers stowing their gear away until tomorrow while others were making mad dashes to the school buses that waited parked out front. As Sue walked to her locker Monika, Janie, and two other girls from her class came up from behind her.

"Hey, Sue," said Monika. "Tell me, are you and Kirby Carson going steady now?" she asked as the other girls laughed in the background.

"It's just a project, Mon. It's not like we signed a marriage license or anything. Besides, how bad can it be? If you ask me, he'd be pretty cute if he cut that hair and occasionally wore something different from that old jean jacket all the time," said Sue as she attempted to play the whole thing off as no big deal all the while inside she was dreading every moment of being paired up with Kirby. The last thing that she wanted to do was to let Monika know that she was getting under her skin. She wouldn't give her that satisfaction.

"If you say so," replied Monika in a way that let the other girls know that she would never stand for the pairing. "Janie and I will be researching George Washington. He was the first and best president.

I'm sure that's why Mr. Walton assigned him to us. I guess I just got lucky with my partner and my president."

"Yeah, we did," added Janie for no other reason than to show Monika that she was on her side.

"Sue. Hey, Sue! Wait up," said a crackled and awkward sounding voice from the crowd of students that crammed the hallway behind her.

"Well, here comes your new boyfriend now," laughed Monika. "We'll just leave you two lovebirds alone," she said. Janie and the other girls laughed as they all walked away down the hall.

"Sue?"

She heard her name and then felt a tap on her shoulder. She turned to see Kirby standing right behind her. His hair was slightly messed and his jeans were faded more from wear and tear than from being in style. He had on a black t-shirt that was emblazoned with a picture of some long haired rock n roll band from a million years ago. The band name was difficult to read as his ever present jean jacket obscured her view.

"Um hi. I'm, uh, Kirby. Kirby Carson. I'm your project partner from American History class," he said as he squirmed in place and tugged at the collar of his jacket with his left hand. His palms were a sweaty mess and his heart raced in his chest. He wiped his right hand on his jeans and then extended it in her direction.

"Uh, yeah," she replied and reluctantly took his hand. She briefly shook it then wiped her own hand off on her pants. "We were just paired up like five minutes ago. I remember who you are."

"Well, yeah. Um, well, I just wanted to say hi and, uh, see, well, when you wanted to get together to start some of the research on the Big T. J. Uh, you know, Thomas Jefferson. His initials are--"

"Yeah, I get it," replied Sue. "Anyway, I'm busy after school today helping my friend Monika with her campaign. She's running for school president you know? I'm her campaign manager. I'm free tomorrow. I guess it's easier for you to come to my house then it is for me to go to yours. So, maybe you can plan on coming over tomorrow and we can get started then. Okay?" said Sue and cringed at the idea of having Kirby Carson over to her house, but she could only imagine the horrors that would await her if she went to Kirby's house. She felt that this was the lesser of two evils.

"Um, yeah, sure. Okay. I--," stumbled Kirby with his reply.

"I have to run now and catch up with my friends, but here is my email address," she said as she handed Kirby a scrap of paper that she had written upon. "I guess you can write me tonight if you have any ideas. Then we can talk tomorrow--after school. Okay?

"Oh, sure," he said. He took the scrap of paper and put it into his pocket. "I don't have--I mean, right now we don't--"

"Okay. Like I said, I have to run now, but email me if you need--I mean if you want to tonight. Bye," said Sue as she quickly turned around and ran down the hallway to catch up with Monika and the other girls.

"Yeah. Sure. Um, bye," said Kirby to no one as Sue faded into the crowd of other teens that were gathered in the hallway. "What I was going to say is that we don't have a computer at our house right now," he whispered to himself as he pulled at the tattered collar of his jean jacket. He pulled it as far as it would stretch as if to hide inside it like a turtle in a shell.

It was then that someone gave all of his books a jab from behind. The books burst out from under his arm and scattered onto the floor with a thud.

Meet Henry Martin

"Loser," shouted Henry Martin; the reigning school bully. He turned and cocked his fist back as if he was going to hit Kirby, then laughed when Kirby had flinched and put his hands up for cover. "Loser!" he yelled one more time before he ran down the hallway with his band of merry troublemakers.

"Yeah smelly loser!" One of the boys from Henry's group shouted as they all run past Kirby.

Kirby lowered his hands and looked out from behind his shaggy bangs. The other kids in the hallway had stopped what they were doing and were focused on Kirby and the books that lay scattered at his feet. He calmly bent down and gathered his belongings and scooped them up under his right arm. He slowly stood up. Again, he pulled the collar of his jean jacket toward his face, and walked silently in the direction of the exit.

#

In the school library, Monika and a handful of other girls were gathered around a table in the back of the room.

"Yeah, but he's Kirby Carson, Janie," said Monika. "He's the smelliest, grossest boy in the school. And…he's a weirdo. He simply makes my skin crawl," she exclaimed.

One of the other girls leaned in closer to the center of the table and whispered, "My Mom said that she saw Kirby's Mom at the store paying for food with an EBT card. They're on the food stamps!"

"Hi, Monika," said Sue as she joined the others at the table. "What did I miss?"

"We we're just talking about your new boyfriend, Kirby," replied Monika with a snicker. "I don't know what you see in him," she laughed. The other girls laughed accordingly. "I'm kidding with you Sue. Seriously though, is he a good kisser?" Monika joked loud enough to draw a long exaggerated *Shhhhhhh!* from the librarian.

"Girls, please settle down," requested the librarian in a firm, but hushed voice.

Sue sat down in one of the available seats at the table. "Like I said," she whispered. "He's not my boyfriend. He's my project partner." The other girls snickered quietly. "I'm not sure what to do. Do you think that maybe I should talk to Mr. Walton and get a new partner?"

"Sue, you should fake death! If I were you, I'd do anything to get out of working with that *loser*," said Janie as she looked at Monika for approval.

"Not my problem, Susie," Monika said.

"Yeah, I just thought--"

"Anyway, girls," interrupted Monika. "Let's get back to planning my campaign. We should begin by making a list of my many qualities that would ideally make me the logical choice to be the next president. Then we will make a list of the inadequacies of my opponents. You know, stuff that I can use to bury them."

The girls began to make suggestions and do their best to appease Monika. Together, they worked on the campaign for almost hour. When the hour had ended the girls slowly began to excuse themselves one by one from the table until only Monika, Janie, and Sue remained.

"I think we made a lot of progress today. Don't cha think so, Mon?" asked Sue.

"I guess, but we really need to get things in gear. I don't plan on just winning; I want to crush the other candidates, especially that Myron Albertson nerd. He went to the same summer camp as me and he was just really creepy and everything. He was always following me around and stuff."

"Yeah, I heard that you liked him or something like that," added Janie.

Monika glared in Janie's direction. "Get your facts straight. He liked me, but I choose to date more handsome, respectable boys. Something that Myron could only dream of being."

Janie and Sue looked at each other; both tried hard not to laugh.

"Janie, are you sure you can be serious long enough to be helpful to this team? If you're so distracted by the likes of *Myron Albertson*, then maybe there is no room for you on my campaign squad."

11

"Sorry, Mon. I was just repeating something that --" Janie said trying to explain what she really meant and to sooth Monika at the same time.

"I know what you said and I asked that you get your facts straight before you spew such bogus lies. Consider yourself warned," scolded Monika.

"Okay," said Janie while she gathered up her books. She picked up her backpack in one hand and pushed in her chair with the other. "I have to go. My mom is probably waiting out front for me. Bye."

"Bye, Janie. See you tomorrow." Sue said. Janie flashed a quick wave before she made a beeline to the exit of the library.

"I hope that she can stay focused. I will win this presidency with or without her help," Monika replied just loud enough for Janie to hear.

"I'm sure she'll be okay. She was just adding to the conversation. Plus, it might be good to know what kind of mud that some of the other candidates might try to fling at you. You know, get the inside scoop on what they are thinking so you can respond positively. Janie's cool," Sue interjected. "She means well and wants to help you win."

"I guess," replied Monika still staring at the door where Janie had already exited. She then turned and focused her attention on Sue. "So, now that it's just the two of us, what are you going to do tomorrow?"

"What do you mean?" Sue asked pretending not to know what Monika was getting at.

"You know, that whole thing with Kirby Carson. I mean, really, are you going to stay partnered up with him? I'm not sure that even *my* popularity could survive a hit like that. He's been here for like five years and he doesn't have one friend. Don't you think that is just a little freaky? Like I once heard that he went to Matt McCormick's birthday party a few years ago and just sat there in the kitchen and didn't go outside to play any of the games or anything; not even when the magician showed up. Supposedly, after he left Matt's mom found bugs on the chair where he had been sitting. She got so disgusted that she had to throw the entire dining room table and chairs out."

12

"I heard that the party was a flop and they were getting rid of the old furniture as part of a makeover on the kitchen. Who likes magicians anyway? It's like, tell me how you did the trick and maybe I can sit through that stuff a little longer. Maybe the cake was really good and he was getting his fill." Sue said as she began to laugh at the thought of someone eating piece after piece of birthday cake until their insides were bulging with cake and frosting. Then having to be rolled outside to the curb and loaded onto a big truck in order to get home.

"Whatever. Either way, you should think about getting a new partner. He'll be death to your social life!"

"I guess. Well, I should be headed out. Um, I think that my Dad will be here soon to pick me up or I might just walk home or something. I guess I'll see you tomorrow."

With that, the girls closed up their binders and headed for the exit.

#

Several miles away Kirby stepped off of the city bus and up the old stone steps in front of the public library. He grabbed the old, tarnished handle of the large wooden door and swung it open with a slight grunt. The moldy smell of ancient books whirled into his nose and stung his brain. Although the library had tried its best to stay modern by adding several computer terminals throughout the study nooks, there was just no getting rid of the smell of old books. Kirby pretended not to like the smell and crunched up his nose as if to say, "What is that horrid smell?" when he saw one of the many librarians, but in reality he enjoyed the scent. He liked the mixture of modern technology and old school charm. The library was a home away from home of sorts for Kirby. Even before they installed the computers Kirby enjoyed frequenting the library on an almost daily basis. On most days he would end up seated at one of the study cubicles gathering information on an astronaut or famous pilot or simply reading a new adventure story from the fiction section. Generally, the study cubicles were reserved for students researching class projects, but the librarians knew Kirby by name and liked him enough to bend the rules.

Once he was inside the library he walked down the long line of computer terminals until he found one that was a good distance away from anyone else. He set down his bag, took his coat off, and slung it over the back of the chair. Before he sat down and got to work he went over to the vending machines and grabbed himself a candy bar and a nice cold soda. He went back to the desk and sat down in front of the computer.

The computer was already on and the screen displayed the library login page. He typed in his user name and password and was then greeted by the Welcome screen. The left column of the screen contained his favorite links and the books that were currently checked out in his name. The right column had a list of suggested links and books recommended by the librarians. Down the middle was the library news that listed upcoming events and a complete list of new books. Kirby clicked on the "Search" link and then typed in the name "Thomas Jefferson". He sifted through the many results and made note of the links that he thought might be contain useful information that he could use for the project.

Several minutes later the librarian came by and glanced over his shoulder to see what was on the computer monitor. "Hi, Kirby," She said. "Researching a new adventure hero of yours?"

"Hi, Ms. Lancaster. No, actually I'm gathering information on Thomas Jefferson for a new class project that I've been assigned."

"Very well. Tell your Mother I said hello, wont you?"

"I will, Ms. Lancaster," said Kirby.

Before he realized it, more than an hour had passed. Kirby had begun to get hungry and his brain was numb with all of the new information that he had obtained. He had gotten off to an excellent start on his project and decided to call it quits for the day.

"*Email me with any ideas.*" Sue had said to him; her voice bounced around in his head. He wondered if she really meant that or if she had just said anything that she could to get out of the conversation with him. Then he remembered the scrap of paper in his front pocket; the one that Sue had written her email address on. The fact that she had taken the time to write it out for him made him think that she really did want him to email her. He reopened the web browser and went to Gmail.com. Aside from the occasional Star Trek forum that he belonged too, he really hadn't had much of a use for an

14

email account. He clicked the link to create a new email account; one that he intended to use for school purposes only like emailing Sue with. While he thought about creating an email address with some flashy space-themed name, in the end he settled for plain old KirbyCarson@gmail.com.

Kirby drafted several different versions of his email to Sue before he finally settled on a simple greeting followed by a list of links that he recommended that they use for research. His email was boring and plain, and lacked any hint that he was in fact a teenager. It read more like an adult had written it and was free of emoticons and abbreviations. Finally, with much anxiety, he typed in her email address -- SusanAliceAndrews@gmail.com -- held his breath and clicked the SEND button. In a flash his email was gone; it cruised through the Internet at the speed of light headed for Sue's INBOX. He exhaled and felt drained from his research.

Kirby logged off of the computer, gathered his belongings, and headed for the door.

"Goodnight, Kirby Carson," said Ms. Lancaster.

"See ya, Ms. Lancaster," replied Kirby with a smile.

Kirby heaved the large library doors open and walked outside. He trotted down the steps and walked over to the bus stop where several people were already waiting for the bus to arrive. He walked over to an empty bench and began to sit, but stopped and offered the open spot to an elderly woman.

"Thank you." The woman said as she inched her body downward onto the bench. "It feels good to rest my old bones, but you don't have to stand. There's room enough for you and me both," she said as she patted the empty space next to her.

Kirby smiled and slowly sat down next to the old woman. He smiled again as he shifted his body around to get comfortable; being careful as to not bump up against the woman.

"I won't break and I don't bite," the woman laughed.

Kirby flashed an awkward smile and felt his face burn with embarrassment.

"I'm Greta," said the woman. "I'm on my way across town to visit a friend of mine." She held out her hand in front of Kirby. He looked down at her old, wrinkled skin and hesitantly raised his hand to hers. One of the few things that Kirby's dad had taught him was that you can judge a person by the way they shake hands and Greta had a nice handshake, especially for an old lady. He'd expected her hand to be cold and clammy and instead found that she was warm to the touch with a rather firm grip. Kirby smiled.

"Kirby, Kirby Carson," he said. "I'm on my way home. I was gathering some information for a class assignment on Thomas Jefferson."

"Sounds exciting," replied Greta.

"I guess so," said Kirby. "This isn't my first report. As long as my project partner can pull her own weight then we should do okay."

"Oh, you're working with a lady friend? That sounds nice." The woman smiled.

"I guess." Kirby said and again felt his face warm.

"Well, she must be a cute one," said Greta.

"I guess. She's okay. Um –"

"Well, she's lucky to be partnered with such a handsome young man," Greta added.

"I guess." Kirby said again.

From their left was the sound of brakes squeaking as the bus pulled up to the bus stop.

"Well, this is my bus." Kirby said.

"It was a pleasure to have met you, Kirby Carson. Good luck with your report," Greta said as Kirby boarded the bus.

Kirby popped some coins into the slot and walked to the back of the bus. He found an empty seat and sat down. He slid close to the window and put his backpack on the aisle seat and hoped that no one would sit next to him.

He felt the bus lurch forward as they pulled away from the bus stop. He looked out the window at the old woman sitting on the bench. "*She called me handsome*," he said to himself. His own grandmother used to call him handsome. He wondered if it were just something that grandmas said. No one his age ever said anything like that to him.

As the bus drove on his eyes watched as the blur of the outside world flashed by. He thought of the project and Sue Andrews and of the million and one different scenarios that might play out before this project was completed. His mom always said that he thought too much and that he should just let things happen. He knew that she was right, but still, it didn't stop his mind from churning up a storm of unknowns.

The Ronster Romp Revisited

"Dad, I'm home," shouted Sue as she walked in through the front door of the white ranch style house.

"I'm in the kitchen, Sue," yelled out Sue's dad.

Sue shed her backpack and let it fall to the floor in the hallway and then walked into the kitchen where she saw her Dad sitting on a bar stool. He was eating a sandwich as he thumbed through a thick stack of papers.

"How was your day, sweetie?" he asked as she came up and gave him a quick hug.

"It was okay I guess," Sue said as she glanced around the kitchen and slowly shuffled her feet around. Suddenly she remembered the bag of cookies on the counter. She grabbed the bag, opened it up, and snatched a handful of cookies.

"It doesn't sound like it was okay. Did anything happen today?"

"Do we have any more milk," She asked as she made her best attempt to elude the question.

"Did you look in the refrigerator?" Mr. Andrews said with a slight chuckle.

Sue looked at him and rolled her eyes. She'd had such a bad day and desperately wanted to tell someone about every detail. She wanted to scream to the world how frustrated her best friend Monika had made her and about this stupid project and her stupid project partner Kirby Carson, but at the same time she didn't say a word. She'd wanted to explain it to him, but not only couldn't she not find the right words, but she dreaded that somehow the conversation would turn into the same old speech about the birds and the bees and growing up. Her dad always found a way to work *that* talk into the conversation. It was awkward at best and Sue did her best to avoid it at all costs even if it meant harboring her frustrations to herself.

"Are you sure there's nothing bothering you?"

Silence

Sue fumbled some more with the bag of cookies and directly ignored the question.

"Yeah," he said. "Your mother was always better at this type of thing than I was. Well, anyway, you know you can always talk to me, right?"

"Yeah--I know," Sue replied in a quiet voice. In her mind she envisioned coming home after a rough day at school and curling up on her bed. Her mom would always know when something was wrong. She'd come in and sit on the bed with her and run her fingers through Sue's hair. Sue wouldn't need to say a thing. Mom always did all of the talking until things just worked their way out. That was before three summers ago when her Mom had died after a long battle with cancer. Since then it had been just her and her dad. She knew that Dad did his best, but sometimes she needed a Mom to talk to, especially when it came to boys. Whether they were cute or yucky Mom always made it an easy topic to talk about. "I know, Daddy." She said much louder this time letting him know that she appreciated his efforts.

Sue found the milk on the top shelf of the fridge where he said it would be and poured herself a glass. She then sat down next to her dad at the counter.

"Whatcha reading," she asked and looked at the stack of important looking paper that sat before him.

"Well, this is a contract," he replied as his fingers thumbed the edges of the stack.

"A contract for what," Sue questioned. "Are we buying a new house?"

"Hardly," he replied. "It's much better than that; it's a recording contract. The old production company, you know, the one that I was with when I released The Ronster Romp, wants me to re-record the old tune as part of a new full length album." Mr. Andrew's smile beamed from ear to ear.

"Daddy, no not that corny song again," exclaimed Sue. "I love you Daddy, but that song is too weird."

19

"Well, that weird and corny song helped to pay for the house you live in today. The record company thinks that after 20 years people are ready for a remake and they want me to be the one to remake it. This could be that second big break that I've been waiting for."

"That's nice, Daddy. Please don't play that song when my friends are around," Sue said with a laugh.

Kirby Dreams Big

A big dirty bus with an advertisement for perfume splashed on the entire side pulled up to the bus stop and came to a halt. The folding doors opened and Kirby walked down the steps onto the sidewalk. He made a right turn and began the walk home.

He approached a tall blue duplex. The rusted hinges on the old gate at the end of the walkway gave way with a loud creak when Kirby pushed it open. He walked down the old cracked concrete sidewalk to a stairway on the side of the house. He grabbed the old wooden railing and went down the steps two at a time until he reached the door of the basement apartment. Kirby opened the door just as his Mom whisked by in front of him.

"Oh, Kirby I'm glad that you're home. Have you seen my other shoe? I'm late for my second shift and I can't find my other shoe." His mother was an aging woman with a decent figure. Her normally long wavy brunette hair was restrained in a tight bun on the top of her head.

"It's right here, Mom," said Kirby as he handed her the misplaced shoe. "Ms. Lancaster from the library told me to tell you hello."

"You were at the library again? Your head is going to explode if you don't do something other than study and read all the time. You need to get out with your friends more, Honey."

"Yeah. I'll have to do that sometime," he said in a muffled voice and he looked down at the brown shag carpet.

His mom stopped and put her hands on either side of his head and pulled him into her. With a loud exaggerated *SMOOCH* sound she planted a big kiss on his forehead. "You're a good kid, Kirby. Don't ever change." She stepped back and slipped on her other shoe. "There's money on the counter. Order yourself some Chinese and get me an egg roll. I'll eat it when I get home. I shouldn't be late tonight. I gotta run. Love you," she said and then walked out the door and into the night.

Kirby kicked off his sneakers, hung his jacket on the coat rack near the door, and sat on the couch gazing at the wall. He thought about his project with Sue and about his encounter with Henry Martin and all of the other kids who tease him and make fun of him. His thoughts turned into a daydream in which he finally got the upper hand on Henry and put him in his place in front of the whole school. In his daydream, he knocked Henry down with one well-placed punch, a la Chuck Norris. Henry would be nervous that Kirby would finish him off. Kirby would cock his fist back and fake one last punch. Henry would wince, begin to cry, and maybe pee his pants. The entire school body would laugh at Henry. They'd carry Kirby off on their shoulders and all the kids would call Henry "Baby Huey" for the rest of the school year--maybe even the rest of his life. All of the girls would want to be Kirby's girlfriend. He'd have them line-up like the girls from Deal or No Deal and one by one he'd walk among them. After making them wonder who he was going to pick, he'd tap one on the shoulder. She'd turn around and kiss him.

More thoughts and dreams filled Kirby's head as he drifted off to sleep on the couch.

Later that evening, he was still asleep on the couch when the sound of the door opening and his mom returning home from work startled him from his light slumber.

"Kirby, wake up, honey. Did you eat?" She said and gently shook his shoulder.

Kirby rubbed the sleep from his eyes and said, "No. I guess--I guess I fell asleep."

"That's all right. I got off work early. We still have time to grab something to eat. Want to walk down to the pizza parlor and get a slice," she asked as she turned and headed back toward the door.

"Nah, Mom. I think I'm just going to go to bed. I have a big project to work on tomorrow and I'm beat. Thanks anyway," he said.

She turned back around and for the second time that night she grabbed him by the head and planted a big wet kiss on his forehead. "Okay, Sweetie sleep tight."

Kirby got up and walked into his bedroom. Without even turning on the light, he changed into a pair of sweatpants and crawled under the blankets. For a few moments he stared at the ceiling and imagined race cars and rocket ships. His thoughts turned to dreams and soon enough he was asleep once again.

Miles away Sue sat at the computer in her bedroom and opened her email. There were four new emails--one from Kirby Carson.

Mr. Andrews The Nerdball

KNOCK KNOCK

"Come in," said Sue, as her eyes remained focused on the computer monitor. She heard the door open behind her and the familiar voice of her father.

"Hey. I just wanted to come in and say good night."

"Okay Daddy. I'm just checking my email before I go to bed." Sue said with a laugh.

"What's so funny?" He asked.

"Nothing. You wouldn't understand," she replied.

"Are you sure? I've done a few things here and there in my life and I actually know a thing or two about funny stuff." Mr. Andrews smiled uneasily.

Sue sighed loudly.

"Okay, I get it. You don't need to tell me twice. Good night, Susie-Q," he said and turned back to face the open door.

"Dad wait a minute," Sue said reluctantly and turned her stare away from the monitor to face him. "It's this guy at school."

"Oh, a boyfriend! Wooooo," He teased.

"Forget it, Daddy." Sue started to turn back in the direction of the computer screen.

"I'm sorry. I'll be quiet," he said and sat down on the edge of her bed.

"It's this boy at school and he's NOT a boyfriend. He's kind of nerdy and I got partnered up with him for a class project. I tried to blow him off in the hallway today. For some reason I gave him my email address and he wrote me tonight."

"Wait, so you're not interested in this so-called nerdy boy, but you gave him your email address? What am I missing here?"

"Daddy! Just listen. Sheesh! We got assigned partners today and he's already emailed me with two pages of ideas. It's like he went straight home and did nothing but research. I told you he was nerdy and everyone makes fun of him. This is going to be the worst thing ever."

24

"If by the worst thing ever you mean that you'll get a good grade on this assignment then I am all for it! You should have him come over to study sometime," Mr. Andrews said with a large sarcastic grin on his face.

"I already invited him to come over to study, but I think I'm going to ask for a different partner tomorrow anyway. Monika already called him my boyfriend and people think I'm with him," she sighed as her shoulders and head slunk downward.

"Sue, do you really care that much what people think?"

She raised her head and rolled her eyes.

"All I'm saying is that maybe you should give the kid a chance. And seriously, if the worst thing that happens is that you get a passing grade, then it's all worth it. Who knows, maybe he's a real nice person and you guys will hit it off. You know I was a geek at one time too, but look at me now," he said while hitting his chest in exaggerated motions like an ape. "Me big hunky ape man now! Oooo Ooooo Aaaah aaah!"

"Daddy, you're weird!"

"Good night, darling. And this kid, what's his name again?"

"Kirby, Kirby Carson."

"Yeah, well give Kirby some slack. Maybe he just needs a friend to be nerdy with you big nerd ball!" He said and threw two stuffed animal dogs playfully in her direction. "Don't stay up all night instant messaging Monika. Her dad may not care that she stays up all night on the computer, but yours does. Lights out in 20 minutes."

The Library

"Alright class pay attention. Today we'll be going to the library to begin research on your projects," instructed Mr. Walton. "When we get there please split off with your project partner and the two of you grab a study booth. And remember, it's the library so you need to keep the chatter to a dull roar," he said and then scanned the classroom for anyone that might not be paying attention. The class then got up in unison and followed Mr. Walton into the hallway where they went off in route to the library.

"So, when are you going to ask Mr. Walton for a new partner?" Monika whispered to Sue as they walked down the hallway.

Sue looked around to make sure Kirby wasn't within earshot and said, "I don't know. I talked to my dad and he said to give it a shot working with Kirby. Hey, I figure that I'll be able to kick back while he does the work and I get the grade."

"Brilliant," Monika exclaimed. "And after you get the good grade maybe the two of you can go to the same college and then get married and have little nerd babies." Monika grabbed Janie by the arm and walked away.

The class entered the library and two-by-two the teens paired off to find available study booths. Reluctantly, Sue walked slowly in the general direction of Kirby and then, without saying a word, they silently wandered over to a study booth together.

They both sat down and after a few minutes of silence Kirby spoke. "Did you get my email?" He asked shyly.

"Yeah, what did you do just sit at home and research last night," Sue said in a slightly condescending manner.

"Um, well--I--I just know a little about this stuff. I mean, you know, I don't sit at the library and research or anything--ya know," Kirby replied. He could feel his neck getting hot as he began to feel awkward around Sue. Without realizing it his hand had reached up and he began to tug at the collar of his jean jacket. "So, um, I hear that your friend Monika is running for class president."

"Yeah. If her dad had his way she would be president of the school and then 20 years from now she'd be president of the country."

"That's cool I guess--I mean–." Kirby's words stumbled their way out of his mouth.

"Are you two researching or just chit chatting," asked Mr. Walton.

"No. Mr. Walton. I mean, yes, we're–we're researching," Kirby replied as he tugged harder on his jacket collar.

"Yeah, look," Sue said and held up the printout of Kirby's email. "We got a head start last night and we're making good ground."

"OK. Great! But let's keep the voices down," Mr. Walton said and then he walked off to another group of classmates.

Out of the corner of her eye Sue could see that Monika had been attempting to get her attention. Sue looked over at Monika. Her lips were puckered as she made 'kissy' faces back at her and then mouthed, *"You Love Kirby."* She used her fingers to trace the shape of a large heart in the air in front of her.

Kirby turned his head just in time to see what Monika was doing. He turned back to Sue and said, "It's alright. I know the other kids make fun of me. You can laugh if you want. It is kind of funny sometimes."

Embarrassed and tongue-tied Sue attempted to talk, "Um, No. We just--I mean they are--Yeah, Monika is kind of funny sometimes. We don't make fun of you; it's just that– "

RINNNNNNNNNGGG!

"OK, that's the bell people. Class is over. On Monday be sure to bring your project outlines for me to review. Have a good weekend," said Mr. Walton.

"I gotta run to my next class. Um, you still wanna come over to study tonight," asked Sue as she gathered up her books, stood up, and began pushing in her chair.

"I dunno. I--I think I gotta go right home after school and help my Mom. Maybe some other time," said Kirby. He got up from the study booth, headed over to the library doors, and then disappeared into the hallway.

Pizza and the Reply

"Sue-be-do-bee-doooo! What do you want on this pizza," asked Mr. Andrews.

"Extra cheese! Oh--and mushrooms! No pepperoni!"

"Alrighty," he said. It was a common occurrence that Sue and her dad made pizza at home. While Sue was at school her dad would pick up some dough and pizza toppings from the local deli. When she got home Sue would roll out the dough while dad fired up the oven.

Mr. Andrews handed Sue a bag of cheese and a bin of fresh mushrooms. "Load it up, Baby!" He laughed. "Extra cheese and mushrooms it is!"

"How's that contract thing going," asked Sue as she spread thick layers of cheese over the dough and red pizza sauce.

"Good! It sounds like I might have to fly out to California in a couple weeks to meet with some big wigs. Maybe take in a Dodger's game and hope for the best. How's that project of yours going? Did you request a new partner today?"

Sue stopped spreading the cheese and shook her head. "Nah. I decided that I should stick it out. It's going to be a pain though. Monika is constantly making fun of me and-"

"Maybe she likes him?" He nudged Sue and raised his eyebrows.

"Hardly Dad! He's definitely NOT her type! I don't think he's anyone's type! I feel bad for him. Everyone picks on him and – "

"Do you pick on him? Come on, Sue-be-doo. Do you?" He stopped spreading the pizza toppings and looked at her in a serious manner.

"Not really, but– "

"But," interrupted Mr. Andrews, "you do laugh when the other kids laugh, right?"

"Well yeah. Kind of," She said as her feet began to cross over each other. She knew what he was going to say and already she had felt ashamed.

Her dad shook his head in disgust. "You know that's not cool. It's tough to fit in. I should know. I wasn't always the cool dad that you see now. I went through a very awkward stage where I grew my

28

hair long and people thought that I looked like a girl. I took a lot of teasing from the other kids, but I felt that since I was being myself that nothing else mattered. Anyway, like I said before, give him some slack." He could tell by the look in her eyes that she knew what she had done was wrong. "You never know. Maybe he is cool or rad or hip or whatever you kids say these days," he said and laughed.

"I guess. I mean, he is smart. And I think that he likes music," she said with a slightly energized tone in her voice. "He wears this jean jacket, like all the time. Oh, and the front, the front has all these buttons on it of different rock bands. The back has this really big patch of some band called Led Zep–"

"Led Zeppelin? Kirby likes Led Zeppelin? They were awesome! Ask him if he has Led Zeppelin IV. Very cool album," said Mr. Andrews. The two of them continued to load the pizza with toppings.

"Well, you could have asked him yourself. I invited him over tonight, but he said that he was busy helping his mom or something like that."

"Maybe he can come over this weekend and you guys can get more research done. It wouldn't hurt you to study more often. By the way, who told you to stop putting cheese on that pizza? More cheese!" He laughed out loud as he popped a mushroom into his mouth.

Later That Night

Sue sat slumped in her chair while she played on her computer and checked her email. Monika had written to her and included a bunch of campaign slogans for Sue to read and she also had sent a picture that she had made of a couple kissing. She had pasted Sue's class picture over the girl's head and Kirby's face on the guy's head. She groaned as she read the campaign slogans and just shook her head wondering how Monika could be so immature at times. She looked in her INBOX and saw the old email from Kirby. She opened it and clicked REPLY--

Kirby,

Sorry about today. My dad said that you should come over and wants to know if you have four led zep CDs? Call me tomorrow and let me know—

ttyl

Sue

Sue typed in her phone number and thought about clicking the SEND button. She hesitated for a minute before reluctantly sending the email. "*Maybe he won't check his email,*" she thought to herself. She wanted to give Kirby a chance to be friends, but she also wondered what Monika would say. Sue always said that she didn't care what other people thought, but often she found herself wondering what Monika would do if Kirby started to hang around. In her heart she knew that Monika would make life very difficult and Sue wasn't sure that she could put up with that for very long.

Sue sat in bed watching old movies before she fell asleep with the TV on.

The Call of a Lifetime

"Kirby! If you want to catch a ride to the library with me then you better shake your tail! I can't be late for work," Kirby's mom said as she rushed around the apartment in a mad scramble to get out of the house in time.

"I'm coming. I'm coming!" Kirby yelled out as he bounced into the living room and pulled on one of his socks. He sat on the edge of the couch and pulled the other one on. He then walked over and casually slid his feet into his sneakers. "All ready," he declared.

"OK, then let's go," She said. They both walked outside as Kirby's mom shut and locked the door behind them.

Once Kirby was at the library he found the same terminal that he was at the other day. He put down his backpack, slid out the chair and sat down. Ms. Lancaster walked slowly behind him and glanced over his shoulder. "Hello, Ms. Lancaster," Kirby said. "My mom also said to tell you hello."

"Hello Kirby. Please remember to keep the talking and noise to a minimum," she instructed.

Kirby logged into the computer and thought about doing some more research. On a whim he signed into his newly created email account and expected to find a bunch of spam mail. Forty-three spam and one real email awaited him. *"One must have gotten by the spam filter,"* he thought to himself and laughed until he realized that the email was actually a reply from one susanaliceandrews@gmail.com! His heart skipped a beat as he moved the mouse pointer over the email subject. In a moment of true bravery he took a deep breath and clicked the mouse button to open the email.

The screen displayed the short reply from Sue. Kirby quickly read it and then read it again–this time nice and slow in order to get a full understanding. *"She apologized? She actually apologized! But why does she want to know how many Zepellin CDs I have? Who cares–she's actually making an effort to be a friend--I think,"* He thought to himself. He wasn't exactly sure what to think about what Sue had written and he contemplated clicking the Delete button to trash it all, but instead he opted to print it out for safe keeping. This was a somewhat new feeling for Kirby. Several times in the past he'd

31

been set up by people claiming to be a friend only to be burned when they revealed their true colors, but he always believed in trying again. Plus, he didn't get that feeling from Sue that he usually got from some of the other kids. Quickly he turned off the terminal and raced toward the library exit. On the way he stopped at the printer carousel near the front desk and retrieved his printed copy of Sue's email to him. He paused to read it again and then smiled.

"Kirby Carson! No running in the library. How many times do I have to tell you?" Asked Ms. Lancaster and pointed a finger in his direction. "Slow down."

At Ms. Lancaster's request Kirby changed pace; he had stopped running and had opted for a fast walking motion instead. As soon as he had cleared the front doors he began to sprint in the direction of the bus stop. He waited and he waited and he waited for the bus to arrive. "Come on! Where is this damn bus?!?!" Kirby had said out loud. A middle-aged couple sitting on the bench looked over at him. "Sorry," he said and impatiently looked at his Star Trek watch. *"Where's Scotty when you need him,"* he thought.

Finally, when he just couldn't wait any longer he turned and began to run for home. It was a three mile jaunt from the library to Kirby's house. By the time that he got there he was soaked with sweat and completely out of breath. He jogged inside, tossed his jacket onto the coat rack, and flipped off his sneakers. He grabbed a cold soda from the refrigerator and sat on the couch. His legs burned from the long run and his head pounded with excitement. Gasping for air he tried to take a gulp of his soda; he coughed and gagged as he swallowed the soda down. He stared at the phone as he tried to catch his breath. The phone had never looked so ominous before.

He paced back and forth like a caged lion. He was unsure of how to work up the courage to simply pick up the phone and dial Sue's number. Twice he had picked up the receiver only to put it back down again frustrated at his nervousness. Finally, he mustered up all of his teenage nerve to dial Sue's phone number and hold the receiver to his ear.

"It's ringing," he said aloud to no one "Oh, God! It's actually ringing!" Kirby was petrified with fear, but held steady to the phone.

Suddenly he heard a man's voice in the receiver. "Hello," said the voice.

Kirby assumed that this had to be Sue's dad or brother. "*Did she even have a brother?*" he thought to himself.

"Uh. Hi. Is, uh, is Sue available?" Kirby said. His voice shook uncontrollably.

"Sure. Let me get her. Just a minute."

Kirby could hear the phone being rustled around and mumbled voices in the background.

"Sue, there's a boy on the phone for you! Woooo woooo," said Sue's dad as he handed her the phone. Although the voice was somewhat muffled Kirby heard what he had said and began to panic even more. His eyes darted around the room for his jacket. He remembered that he had actually hung it on the coat rack. He began to walk near it, but stopped short when he heard another voice, a girl's voice, on the other end.

"Stop it Daddy!" Sue said and took the phone from him. "Hello?"

"Ummm. Hi, hi Sue. This is Kirby. Kirby Carson? I. Uh. I got your email and you said to call. You said to call, right?" He questioned. He really needed his jacket. He crept closer and closer on course to the coat rack, but the short phone cord would not let him get close enough to snare it. "Um, can you hold one moment? I need to cough," he said as he faked a cough in the background and in one fell swoop he snatched his jacket and plunged one arm through and then the other. "*Much better,*" he thought to himself. "I'm back. Sorry about that."

"Who is it? Who is it," asked Sue's dad who, at this point, was only mere inches away from her and grinning.

"Daddy, stop it," She said.

"Is it Kirby?" He whispered.

Sue nodded her head yes. "Now go away," She said taking her hand away from the mouthpiece of the phone.

"Um what? Uh, me," Kirby asked as he pulled tightly at the collar of his jacket.

"Oh. Sorry. No. My dad. He's being a dork. Anyway, yeah, like I thought about it last night and thought that maybe if you weren't doing anything you'd want to come over and hang out and work on this outline that we have to have done for Monday. Okay?"

Kirby's fingers released their firm grip on the jacket collar letting it snap back to his shoulder. "Well, ummm--I can't today, but I'm pretty sure that I can tomorrow. My Mom is at work and, like, she would have to drive me and she's already at work and doesn't want me wandering away or anything," Kirby said and again stammered his words.

Sue looked at her Dad who was smiling at her from the other end of the room. He gave her a 'thumbs up' motion before walking out of the room. "Okay. How's noon," she asked.

"That's–that's cool. Oh, why does your Dad want to know how many Led Zeppelin albums I have?"

"I don't know. He's weird. I'll see you tomorrow. Call me before you come over and I'll give you the address. Oh, and Kirby," Sue said as her voice got quiet and more serious. "One more thing; I'm sorry about the other day in the library."

Kirby was speechless. He sat staring at the wall not sure exactly what to say. His mind was a jungle of thoughts and none of them seemed to make it to his lips. He could feel his hand as it reached up for his collar, but he stopped it short and put it in his pocket.

"Kirby? Are you there?"

"Uh. Yeah. That's cool. It was no biggie. So, I'll call you tomorrow. Sue--uh, thanks."

Kirby hung up the phone and sat on the couch in shock. *"Did I just make a study date with Sue Andrews,"* he asked himself. *"What was I thinking? This is great! No, this is awful! Arrrrgh!—"*

The Study Date

All night long Kirby had tossed and turned as he lay in his bed unable to get into a deep sleep. He was anxious and nervous and happy and, well, he was a mixed up mess of emotions!

Sunday morning had finally come and Kirby had ironed out the travel arrangements with his Mom. She was to drop him off at Sue's house on her way to work. When his study date was completed Sue's dad had offered to bring Kirby home. Kirby's mom was overjoyed that he was getting out of the house and out of that moldy smelling library for a change. She was also very pleased that the study date was with a girl.

"Have fun and here's some money, Kirby," Ms. Carson had said when they pulled up in front of Sue's house. She put the car into park and admired the Andrew's home with the long driveway leading up to a set of white columns that flanked the front door. A white picket fence wrapped around the front yard. "*All it needs is a puppy and a tire swing,*" she thought to herself as she smiled.

"What will I need money for?" Kirby asked.

"Maybe you'll get lunch or maybe something will happen and you'll need to call a cab."

"Well, what--what would happen? Maybe--maybe I shouldn't go," he said. His words came out shaky and jumbled.

"It'll be fine. Plus, it's too late to turn back now," she said as she looked and pointed in the direction of a man whom she assumed was Sue's dad as he walked down the driveway to the car.

Kirby's throat made an audible gulping sound as he tried in vain to swallow his fear.

Mr. Andrews walked around to the driver's side window and then squatted down until his head was level with hers. "Hi, I'm Ron, Ron Andrews–Sue's dad." He said and stuck out his hand in her direction.

"Hello, Ron. I'm Wanda Carson--uh, Kirby's mom," She said with a big smile. She took Ron's hand lightly into hers. "It's very nice to meet you. Thank you for letting Kirby come over to study. If it's a problem just have him call a cab if you are unable to bring him home."

35

"Mom," Kirby said from the backseat.

"It's no problem at all. I'll let the kids get their "study" on," he said and made exaggerated quotation marks in the air with his fingers all while he grinned. "And then maybe we'll make some pizza. I should have him home around five. Nice to meet you," Ron Andrews said and gave Kirby's mom a big smile.

Kirby slowly opened the car door and stepped out onto the curb. His hand tugged feverishly on his jacket collar. With his other hand he reluctantly closed the door.

"Have fun," Kirby's mom yelled out the window as she put the car into drive and eased away from the curb.

"So, you must be Kirby. Cool jacket! Sue tells me that you're a big Led Zep fan?"

"Yeah. I didn't bring my CDs though."

"That's cool. I've got them all and then some. A friend of mine helped them in the studio and has a few demo songs on CD that have never been released. Maybe later we can check them out and I can get Sue to burn you a copy--as long as they don't end up on eBay!" Ron laughed as he patted Kirby on the back.

"Seriously? That would be cool and I promise I'd never sell 'em. I wouldn't even let anyone listen to them," Kirby said. His mom lightly honked the horn, waved, and drove away.

Inside, Sue was sitting at the desk in the den. The computer was on and she was IMing Monika. "*OMG! My Dad patted him on the back and now they're laughing. They're coming inside. I gotta go,*" Sue wrote. She closed the IM program and watched as Kirby and her dad entered the house.

"Here, Kirby. Let me hang your coat up," offered Mr. Andrews.

"No, uh, that's okay. I'd rather have it with me." Kirby shoved his hands into the pockets of the jacket as if to wrap himself inside a denim cocoon.

"Okay! You kids have fun! Two hours and we'll make up some pizza," Sue's dad said and then walked back into the kitchen leaving Sue and Kirby alone in the den to study.

"Hi. Uh, wanna sit down?" Sue asked.

"Sure." Kirby replied and sat down on the black rolling office chair that was pulled up next to Sue.

"Want a drink?"

"Um, no thanks." Kirby fidgeted around uncomfortably in his chair.

"Well, I--OK--I, um, took the ideas we had in the library and kind of wrote them here. I figured we could start our outline from that, kinda," said Sue.

"Okay, but actually what you wrote down was just a list of the resources that we've used so far," said Kirby.

"Oh, is that bad?" Sue replied.

"No. We'll actually need those later on. Mind if I type," asked Kirby. His hands eased out of his pockets as he inched closer to the computer--and to Sue.

"Be my guest," Sue replied and slid the keyboard in front of Kirby.

"What I thought we'd do is--," Kirby spun off into a long involved synopsis of how he thought that they should proceed with the project. The whole time that Kirby spoke Sue nodded along in agreement.

"It all sounds good to me," Sue said at the end of it all.

BING

The IM program came back to life and someone with the screen name "pr1nc355m0n1k4" wrote *Is your boyfriend still there??? SMOOCHIE SMOOCHIE!"*

"Arrg! Monika can be such a pain sometimes," Sue exclaimed when the IM window popped up. "She can be such a jerk!" Sue was embarrassed and begged of Kirby to close the IM window.

Kirby reads the message and kind of giggled as he closed the window. "I dunno. She seems kind of cool."

"I mean, she is one of my best friends, but sometimes she is such a butt head," Sue laughed.

"Wanna do something funny to her?" Kirby asked. "I know an IM code that if you send it to her it will make her CD drawer open and then her monitor will shut off for 10 seconds. She'll freak out, but it's totally harmless. It will be hilarious."

"Definitely!" Sue said with excitement.

Kirby typed in the response and clicked the SEND button.

Within one minute the user named "pr1nc355m0n1k4" was gone from the screen. Kirby and Sue laughed. "High five, buddy," Sue said. Kirby reached up and slapped her hand.

"She must have freaked out and shut off her computer." Sue said. "Let's shut that program off so that she can't bother us anymore." Sue reached in front of Kirby, grabbed the mouse and exited from the program. Unexpectedly, the smell of Sue's berry shampoo fluttered into Kirby's nose and slapped his brain.

Kirby's world suddenly seemed to be moving in slow motion. He watched as Sue leaned back into her chair. Her hair fluttered and flitted in the air before coming to rest on her shoulders. She smiled and he watched as two small dimples, one on each side of her mouth, puckered inward on her cheeks. Her teeth were a brilliant white and her lips were a pale pink.

"OK, let's get back at this," Sue said and shattered Kirby's slow motion world. He was now back in reality and tucked firmly inside his jacket.

The Study Date Part 2

"So, Janie said to her that her dad had two jobs," exclaimed Sue.

"No way! She didn't say that to her!" Kirby said and laughed at the joke.

"Hey, is it safe to come in? You kids sound like you're having way too much fun to be studying," Sue's dad said sarcastically.

"Daddy!"

"Sorry, Mr. Andrews we were just finishing up," Kirby explained.

"It's cool. I preheated the oven. You guys still wanna make pizza?" Ron Andrews asked.

"Sure," Sue replied.

Kirby just sat there emotionless looking at the computer monitor.

"Come on, Kirby it's fun," Sue said and grabbed him by the shoulder of his jean jacket. She led him in the direction of the kitchen. Kirby was somewhat reluctant, but followed behind her anyway.

In the kitchen Kirby saw three small circles of dough sitting on flour laid that was spread out on the counter. There was a bowl of pizza sauce, a few containers of toppings, and a big block of cheese next to a large shiny cheese grater.

"I don't really know how to cook. I have some money if you guys wanna order some pizza," Kirby said. One of his hands reached for the wallet in his pocket while the other one tugged at the collar of his jean jacket pulling it slightly over his face.

"It's fun and it's easy, Kirby. Come on. Just jump right in. We promise you don't have to cook, but you might have to do the dishes after," joked Mr. Andrews.

"Daddy! He's being a dork, Kirby. You don't have to do the dishes. Come here. I'll show you how this is done."

"Um, okay--," Kirby said and wandered over near the counter.

"Hey, Kirb, why don't you take that jacket off and relax. We're all cool here. Let me hang that up for you over here. Right near the door where you can see it," Mr. Andrews said and reached out to get Kirby's jacket.

Kirby looked at him. Reluctantly, he slid his arms out of his jacket and handed it to him.

"This is going to be fun, Kirby. I promise," said Sue. The three of them began to slather the dough with sauce and spread out their toppings. Sue grabbed a ladle full of sauce and handed it to Kirby. She put her hand over his and showed him the proper sauce spreading technique. Kirby picked at the toppings and put a couple mushrooms here and a slice or two of pepperoni there. Sue grinned and shoved her hand into the mushrooms and sprinkled them on his sauce-covered dough. Kirby laughed and slowly he began to loosen up. He flung slices of pepperoni onto his pizza like mini Frisbees. At one point he was tossing them at Sue's open mouth until she was able to successfully catch one and then the three of them all high-fived in the middle of the kitchen. When the toppings had been dispersed and the cheese has been added they slide the pizzas into the oven and waited. Sue and Kirby cleaned off the countertop while Mr. Andrews put away the toppings. After a while the oven bell rang signaling that their prized pies were ready. Sue's dad pulled the pizzas from the oven. The cheese had melted and the crust was cooked to a golden brown.

Kirby crunched into his pizza and a long, thin string of cheese extended from his mouth to the slice that he held in his hand. Kirby wiped it away with a napkin. The three of them sat and laughed while they knocked back some soda with their home made pizza.

"Excuse me. I'll be right back." Sue said as she got up from the table and walked out of the room.

They heard Sue as she ran up the stairs and then they heard a door close.

"By the way, Kirby, if you have to go to the bathroom, it's up the stairs to the right. But I'd suggest waiting for a bit now that Susie-Q is up there--or at least bring a match to light." Mr. Andrews said with a joking grin and a wink.

Kirby laughed and snorted at the joke. He took a deep breath to control his laughter. Sue and her dad had made Kirby feel very comfortable in their home. Kirby smiled through his sauce and cheese filled mouth and for once he felt happy about making a new friend. Like some crazy infectious laughing disease, Kirby began to chuckle again for no real reason. When he was finally able to control his laughter and could talk again he said, "Mr. Andrews, can I ask you a question?" Kirby's tone had turned serious as he looked at Mr. Andrews.

Sue's dad set down his slice of pizza and wiped his mouth with a napkin. "Sure, Kirby, what's on your mind?"

"Sue says you're pretty cool and you're a musician and all. You seem like a cool guy and, well, like--uh, did you ever get picked on in school?"

At first Ron Andrews was startled by the question. He hadn't expected something so serious to be asked. He quickly gained his composure. "Well, sure I did! Who didn't? That's part of being young."

"Yeah, but, like, was it all the time--every day?" Kirby had begun to feel the urge to go get his jacket.

"Well, I dunno. It was a long time ago. Is this something maybe you should ask your mom or dad? I mean, I'm sure that they have good advice to offer."

"My dad's gone and my mom doesn't understand things. I just thought that you were probably the cool guy at school and no one ever picked on you. Maybe you could help--or--uh--I'm sorry--I--."

Sue's dad could see Kirby fidget in his chair and cut him off, "Me? The cool guy? Kirby, buddy, I was so NOT the cool guy in school! All I did was sit inside my house and play my cello. My mom wouldn't let me play sports and my dad worked all the time. I rarely saw him. So, I'd sit inside and play that cello while all the other kids were outside playing. In high school I switched to electric guitar and started singing. I was a one-man band in my bedroom," he said and laughed. This made Kirby smile a little. "I played along with all the great albums I had. It wasn't until college that things changed. I was in a new place with a new set of people--and I just stepped out of my shadow."

"Really? So there is hope for me too?"

"Kirb, there's hope for everyone. Don't get down on something that a few knuckleheads do. Trust me on this that they all do goofy things too! If you keep putting your best foot forward you'll eventually get to someplace good!"

"Thanks, Mr. Andrews," Kirby said as his attention went back to the slice of pizza that sat on his plate in front of him.

"No problem. And you can call me, Ron. Can I give you one more quick pointer?"

"Uh, I--I guess," Kirby said as he looked up from his plate.

"That's a cool jean jacket you have, but don't be afraid to take it off and show the world the real Kirby; the cool Kirby that is inside that jacket. I'm sure it gets pretty hot in there during the summer. Just don't be afraid and I think you'll see positive things happen. And, hey, feel free to ask me questions anytime."

"Thanks again, Mr. Andrews--I mean Ron," Kirby said with a smile.

"And don't let me forget; when Sue gets back I'll have her burn that CD. We can listen to it on the way back to your house."

"That would be cool," said Kirby.

Later that day

"This is it. It's the one on the right." Kirby directed Sue's dad to stop in front of his house.

"Alright, Kirb. That CD was cool, right?" Ron Andrews asked.

"Yeah, it was awesome," replied Kirby.

"I'll see you tomorrow at school, Kirby," Sue said. "Email me tonight if you get a chance."

"Okay, Sue. Thanks for everything. See ya later." Kirby got out of the car hanging onto his jacket with one hand. "Bye, Sue. Bye, Ron," he said as he ran down the driveway alongside of the house flipping and spinning his jacket in the air.

"Ron? He calls you Ron?" Sue turned and faced her dad.

"Yeah, I had a nice chat with Kirby while you were upstairs peeling the wallpaper in the bathroom."

"Daddy!"

* * * * *

That night at home, Kirby poured through some of his mother's discarded magazines. He was still riding the high of his day spent at Sue's house while he sifted through the magazines in search of a new look. He looked at page after page of tall muscular male models and his euphoria began to fade. *"There's no way that I could ever look like that,*" he thought to himself and put the magazines back. Then he remembered something that Sue's dad had told him, "Be yourself." Kirby smiled and headed off to bed. He lay in bed getting comfortable and thought of ways to be himself. All of the anxiety and excitement of the day made his eyelids very heavy with sleep. Kirby quickly fell asleep and dreamed about being himself.

The Showdown

The school bell rang as Kirby entered the classroom. His hair was styled in a kind of messy, controlled messy kind of way, his jeans were new and crisp, and his jacket was nowhere to be found. He'd pierced his ear and had a clearly visible tattoo of a ninja riding a purple dragon on his bicep.

All of the other students had their eyes locked in on the *new* Kirby Carson. The girls all drooled with delight and the guys were steamed in jealousy. Even Mr. Walton, the teacher, seemed rather impressed with his stylish new looks.

"Well, Mr. Carson. It looks as though you've had an eventful weekend!" Mr. Walton said.

"I sure did," Kirby replied as he nodded his head and winked at Sue and then walked over to his desk. "I sure did."

Mr. Walton began the lesson while the girls were feverishly passing notes back and forth proclaiming their newfound love for Kirby Carson, but there was one girl who Kirby had his eye on and the others would just have to wait and suffer.

Mr. Walton stopped the lesson short and exited the classroom. "I'll be right back," He told the class. Please continue to read Chapter 13 until I return."

Just as Mr. Walton exited the classroom Henry Martin, the school bully, entered and walked to the front of the classroom. He scratched his nails across the chalkboard with a loud ear piercing sound and then turned to face the class.

"Carson! Front and center!" He said with an evil look in his eyes. "Carson! Now!" Henry's fist slapped his open left hand with a loud *THWACK!* "Carson!" *THWACK* went the fist again. "Me and You! Now!" He motioned to Kirby to come join him.

Kirby stood up and strutted bravely to the front of the classroom where Henry awaited. He looked over at Sue and mouthed to her, "I got this."

Once Kirby was at the front of the class Henry Martin wasted no time. He quickly flicked Kirby's new earring and then without warning punched him hard in the stomach. Kirby fell to the ground in a moaning and groaning pile of pain. Henry jumped on him and continued to lob punches into his stomach as the other kids gathered around. With each punch Kirby seemed to lose some of his new *coolness*. First his earring fell out, but before it could hit the ground it disappeared into thin air. Next his hair grew back to its less than stylish, brown and shaggy form. Finally, his tattoo faded until it looked like a chalk drawing done by a first grader and then it completely disappeared altogether.

RIIIIIIIIIINNNNNGGGG! Sounded the class bell. *RIIIIIIIINNNNNNNNNNNGGGGGGG!*

Kirby's alarm clock snatched him from the perils of his dream. His breathing was rapid and he was curled up in a ball under the blankets sweating profusely.

"Oh! It was all just a dream," he said into his pillow. "Henry wasn't beating me up--,"

"Kirby! Time to get up," yelled his mom from just outside his bedroom door.

Kirby got up and made his way into the shower. After he had cleaned up and put on his school clothes Kirby sat in the kitchen eating his breakfast at the table. His mom stood leaning against the doorway.

"So, did you get a lot of studying done at Sue's house yesterday?" she asked.

"Yeah. It was cool. Her dad is awesome."

"He seemed really nice. That's good. And how was Suuuuuuuuuuusiiiiee?" His mom said and reached over to pinch one of his cheeks.

"Mom!"

When he had finished his breakfast Kirby headed toward the door to go and catch his bus.

"Kirby, you're forgetting your jacket," his mom yelled out to him.

"Nah, it's cool. I think I might not wear it today," he said and let the door shut. He walked up the stairs to the driveway and continued out to the street.

Despite his eerie dream Kirby arrived at school that morning with a new spring in his step and a smile on his face. People noticed this too! He passed a group of girls and they smiled, but not in the normal *"What a dork"* kind of way. This was more–genuine.

He walked into class and Mr. Walton gave him a big smile. "Good morning, Mr. Carson! Your smile says that you must have had a good weekend."

"Yeah, I did, Mr. Walton. It was fun," said Kirby. He looked over in the direction of Sue. She was sitting with Monika and Janie and a couple of other girls. Sue waved as the other girls got their first glimpse of the smiling jacket-less Kirby. Janie smiled and gave Kirby a wave.

Monika leaned forward and whispered something into Sue's ear. "Look at the dork," she said. Sue rolled her eyes and motioned for Kirby to come over and sit near them.

Kirby hesitated at first, but walked over to them just the same. He was happy and he felt good, but he knew all too well that just like in the dream that he'd had last night that at any moment it could all come crashing down. All it took was one corny joke or one wrong comment and the other kids would forget the new Kirby and bring the old Kirby back kicking and screaming.

He sat down as Mr. Walton brought the class to attention. He could feel the girls staring holes in his back. He could hear the giggles and the crinkling of paper as notes were passed secretively back and forth. *"Am I being overly paranoid?"* He thought to himself. *"Am I?"*

After what seemed to be the longest class ever the class bell rang and all of the students flooded out into the hallway. Kirby was walking to his locker when Henry Martin rounded the corner. His eyes locked on Kirby and he started to walk in his direction with his posse of monkey jerks following close behind.

"Hey, Nerd! Where's the jacket? Did the garbage men accidentally pick it up because it looked like garbage, loser?" Henry said with a sneer.

"Yeah, ya smelly loser!" One of Henry's followers had squawked.

"I didn't wear it today. Maybe I'll wear it tomorrow or maybe I won't. Okay?" Kirby replied.

"Look, Loser, I don't know what you're up to today, but I suggest that you crawl back into your nerd closet and think about who you're talking to," Henry said and took a step closer to Kirby. Their noses were almost touching. The other students in the hallway all stopped what they were doing and starting to look at the two them.

"Okay, Henrietta!" Kirby said loudly. Small droplets of spittle flew from his mouth and showered onto Henry. Kirby's heart raced as he feared for his life, but he stood his ground--for now.

The hallway erupted into a fit of laughter. The other kids jumped and squirmed in place all while they laughed at Henry. A couple kids pointed and one of them yelled out, "Hey, Henrietta! Your bra strap is showing!"

"This isn't over yet, Nerd," Henry said quietly to Kirby and then turned and ran down the hallway.

Lunch With The Girls

Later that day in the cafeteria

"Kirby? Hey, Kirby! We're over here. I saved you a seat," shouted Sue to Kirby as he exited the food line. He saw her and nodded. He carried his lunch tray that was filled with some sloppy looking meat, a lump of mashed potatoes, and three squares of wiggling Jell-O-like dessert blocks. Kirby turned away from sitting in his usual spot alone near the door next to the trash cans and headed over to the table where Sue, Janie, and Monika were already seated.

Monika rolled her eyes as she saw that he was headed in their direction. "Oh great! I see that your new boyfriend is headed our way. He better not spill anything on me."

"Just give him a chance," Sue pleaded. "He's actually pretty cool. By the way, is your computer acting weird? Maybe the CD drive opened all by itself and the monitor shut off?" Sue laughed as she recalled the trick that Kirby had played on Monika during their study date. "We thought it was funny."

"That was you two? You know you could have really broken my computer really bad!" Monika exclaimed in a hushed voice as she noticed Kirby nearing the table.

"Hi–um–everyone," Kirby stammered as he stood next to the table holding his lunch tray.

"Sit right here. We saved you a spot." Sue told him and pulled out a chair for him to sit in.

"Hi Kirby," Janie said and smiled.

"Hi Kirby. You're looking different today. Have a seat," said Monika. "Sue says that you guys had a great time studying this past weekend at her house. Is that all that you were really doing?" She grinned and paused slightly letting the double meaning sink in. Kirby sat motionless and not sure exactly how to respond. "Oh, Sue also said that you are a whiz with computers. That trick you guys played on me was really funny."

Kirby's face turned a few different shades of red. "I'm sorry. We-uh-I was just joking around. It was–."

Monika cut him off. "No, I thought it was funny! I was laughing and wondering what was going on. It was, like, nuts! After that I logged off and had to go to my riding lesson. But, if you're that good with computers, well maybe sometime if you aren't busy maybe you can come over to my house and show me a few things. Sometimes I feel so stupid on the computer. Maybe you can give me some helpful tips."

"Um, sure anytime. Um, let me know," Kirby said with a smile as a wave of relief crashed over him.

"Well, if Sue here says it's okay, maybe you can come over this weekend? We can make a day of it and you can check out my CD collection." Monika gave Sue a sneer out of the corner of her eye.

"Mon, Kirby and I are project partners not life partners. His weekends are free, unless we have more project stuff to do," Sue said trying not to show that Monika was starting to get under her skin.

"It's, um, cool. We can work out a time. Um, actually, I should be going. I have to study for the test next period. I'll talk to everyone later," Kirby said. He grabbed his lunch tray, got up from the table and walked away. He emptied his uneaten lunch into the trash barrel and exited the cafeteria.

"Sue. Look, Kirby is nice and if you want to date him that is fine with me, but as you know, I am running for President of the school. There might be some issues if I am suddenly seen eating lunch with the school dork. This one time I can forgive you and chalk it all up to charity work, but let's not make it a habit.

"Again, I'm not dating him and why did you just invite him over to your house?" Sue asked very puzzled and somewhat irked by Monika's lecture.

"Look, I was being nice to him. It's called getting votes Sue," Monika said as she made air quotes with her hands, "and as my campaign manager I would expect you to know that. Are you sure that you're on board with this? I mean, Janie can step up and take over if you can't separate your love life from my political life."

"I sure can, Monika. I'm there for you always whenever you need it," blurted out Janie.

"No, um, I can be your campaign manager, Monika. Just realize that he is my project partner and we have to do things together to finish this project."

"Fine, just as long as we are understood." Monika sneered once again in delight.

I Have a Question

That day after school

"Hey, Sue. Wait up," Kirby said as he approached Sue in front of the school. "How do you think you did on that test?"

"I dunno. I think I did okay. What's up?" Sue stopped and adjusted her backpack.

"Not much. I'm headed to the public library to do some more research on the project. Want me to email you later with what I found or I can call you when I get home? Whatever is easier for you."

"Yeah, I -"

"Oh, and I almost forgot. I have to run and catch my bus, but I have something really important that I wanted to ask you. I'll – I'll just call you tonight," Kirby said as he stepped onto the bus and the doors closed behind him. Kirby waved to Sue from his seat as the large faded yellow bus lurched to life and eased out of the parking lot. A small cloud of exhaust shot out the back and engulfed Sue momentarily. Sue coughed and covered her face with her hand.

"Yeah, you do that," Sue said to no one as she coughed some more on the fumes from the bus. "I wonder what he has to ask me." Sue wondered to herself as she fanned away the exhaust and headed off toward the parking lot designated for parents to pick up their children.

HONK HONK

Sue saw her Dad parked just up ahead in his maroon colored Dodge Charger. As she neared the car she let her backpack fall from her shoulder. She opened the passenger side door and tossed her backpack and wind breaker into the back seat. She hopped into the front seat and with a tug snapped the seat belt around her.

"Hey, Susie-Q! How was school today?" Her dad asked.

"Okay, I guess," replied Sue with a sigh.

"Did you see Kirby today?"

"Yeah, I guess," she said while staring aimlessly out the window.

"Is he still around? Does he need a lift home?"

"No, he got on his bus and was headed to the public library to do some more research," she said; her words coming out slow and deliberate.

"You sound a little blue, baby. What's up?" her Dad asked.

"Ah, nothing; it's just the Monday blahs I guess," Sue said as she continued to look out the window. A bird flew down close enough to the car that it looked like it might hit the side closest to Sue, but she barely flinched. Sue took another long, exaggerated breath. Mr. Andrews put the car in "D" and they pulled out of the parking lot into the street. "I dunno. Kirby and Monika and -,"

"Wait, Kirby is dating Monika?" questioned Mr. Andrews.

"Uh, no Daddy! Kirby came to school today looking different and everyone thought he looked good and, like cool and everything. The school bully messed with him and Kirby embarrassed him totally."

"Did they fight," Mr. Andrews asked with a slight look of surprise on his face.

"No, Kirby called him Henrietta and his name is really Henry." Sue's dad let loose with a quick laugh as he pictured Kirby embarrassing the school bully. "Then we went to lunch and Monika kept saying that he was my boyfriend and then she invited him over to her house this weekend so that he could teach her some stupid computer stuff and to look at her CD collection and, like, hang out and stuff."

"So, he's your boyfriend??? You sound jealous–and I'm confused."

"Daddy, he's no one's boyfriend right now. Pay attention. I think Monika embarrassed him because he left abruptly and threw most of his lunch out. He had only taken a couple of bites of his sandwich before he left. Then when he was gone she said that she doesn't really like him and I better not hang out with him because it will ruin her chances of becoming the school President."

"Wow! That was all pretty intense for a Monday."

"Then I saw him after school and he said he was going to call me tonight and that he had something big to ask me."

"Woo hoo! Sounds like Kirby is going to be some one's boyfriend before the day is over!" Mr. Andrew's grinned and laughed a little.

"Daddy--"

Two Surprises

Kirby, alone again at the library, sat at his favorite cubicle researching his class project. It had been a long exciting week of school so far and he had a million things on his mind, but he also knew that he had to make some more progress on his project. He surfed the internet and gathered a lot of useful information. He wondered what Sue was doing. He thought about what had happened at school. He tried to stay focused on his project, but he found his mind wandering more than he liked. It took a while, but after two hours of research he had most of what they needed for the project. He let out a sigh as he'd had enough for one day. He logged into his Gmail account and sent off an email to Sue with the information and to let her know that he would probably call her later that night when he got home. He logged off of the computer, gathered his stuff, and headed outside to the bus stop.

It was a nice day and instead of taking the bus home Kirby decided to walk down to the diner where his mom worked. Her shift ended in about an hour and he thought it would be nice to surprise her at work. He thought that maybe afterward they could go out to grab something to eat and talk or maybe they could just go for a ride.

Kirby walked down the sidewalk. He kicked at small rocks and balanced on the edge of the curb. He got to Donovan Street and made a right. The diner was only four blocks away. As he rounded the corner he bumped into a kid wearing a mismatched and grease stained uniform from a local fast food restaurant. The restaurant was a few blocks down in the opposite direction. "Sorry." Kirby said and glanced over at the kid. At first he didn't recognize him, but then he saw who it was and his eyes widened. It was the class bully, Henry Martin.

"Hey, Loser! That was a real funny joke today. I hope you don't think that I forgot about that already," Henry said as he inched closer and closer to Kirby.

"Look, Henry. I'm sorry man. It just slipped out. No hard fe–," Kirby let out a loud "Uhg!" sound as Henry punched him really hard in the stomach. The blow knocked the wind out of him and Kirby staggered on the curb. He teetered to and fro while he tried to catch his breath.

"Look, Loser, now we're even, but if you even look at me in school I will drop you in front of everyone. If I weren't already running late for my job I'd beat you silly now," Henry said as he gave Kirby one of his patented, big, ugly, decaying tooth smiles. "Don't forget what I said, Loser."

Kirby slumped down and rolled on the dirty sidewalk as he gasped for air. His stomach hurt really badly where Henry had punched him. After several minutes he rolled over onto his backside and propped himself up on the curb. Once he was able to catch his breath he got up on his feet and dusted the dirt off of his shirt and pants. He looked behind him down the street for any traces of Henry, but he was nowhere in sight.

Kirby continued his walk to the diner. As he passed by the flower shop he caught the reflection of himself in the storefront window. His hair was all tussled up and he had a small rip in his shirt. He no longer felt like surprising his mom at the diner, or having a long talk with her, or eating out with her. He just felt like going home and curling up on his bed under the blankets. He turned around and walked back to the nearby bus stop. He sat on the bench and waited for the bus to come; the whole time he thought about his jacket and how alone he felt without it. Soon enough the bus arrived. With a loud *HISSSSS* the door opened and Kirby walked up the steps. He trudged to the back of the bus and sat down alone. He thought about everything that had happened recently with Sue, Monika, and now Henry. It all weighed heavily on his mind.

Once he was at home, he cleaned up and buried his ripped shirt under a bunch of garbage in the kitchen trash can. Just then he heard the clicking of his mom's heals as she walked down the steps outside.

"Hi, Kirby," she said as she opened the door and walked inside. She put her purse down on the table and flipped her shoes off onto the mat near the door.

"Hey, Mom."

"How was school today? Did you have a good day," she asked.

"Yeah, it was okay. I had a test and I think I did okay." Kirby's voice was quiet and almost emotionless.

"Good! Want to go get something to eat," she said and walked past Kirby on her way to her bedroom. The smell of fried food and cigarette smoke trailed behind her.

"Sure," he replied.

"Okay, good. Let me go change and we'll head out. What are you thinking, Chinese maybe?" Her voice tailed off as she entered her bedroom to get changed.

Kirby walked over to the phone and dialed Sue's number. "Uh, Hi Mr. Andrews--I mean Ron. It's Kirby, Kirby Carson. Is Sue there?--Okay, thanks." Kirby said and waited for Sue to pick up the phone.

"Hi Kirby, I got your email. I added the info to the stuff we already had," Sue said quickly as she picked up the phone to talk to Kirby. The tone of her voice was excited, but nervous at the same time.

"Cool."

"So, like, earlier you said that you had something big to ask me?"

"Yeah, yeah. Um, I do. Um, I was wondering if--well, if you--," Kirby's voice became very quiet.

"Kirby, are you there? Kirb? You said you had something big to ask me, right?" said Sue.

"Yeah," he said a little louder. "Um, I was wondering if--well, if you--I don't know how to say this really." Kirby stammered.

"Just spit it out already," Sue giggled.

"Well, things over the weekend went pretty good. It was fun hanging out with you and your Dad and making pizza and all. I don't know if he told you or not, but he answered some questions that I had and we chatted and well, I feel pretty good about myself."

"Okay--and?" Sue began to get more nervous. Her mind raced as she thought about the question that Kirby was leading up to with this conversation.

"Well, then Monday came and everyone seemed to enjoy my new look. Having lunch with you guys was really cool too."

"Why did you leave so quickly then," Sue asked half knowing the answer, but asking the question anyway.

"I dunno. I--I felt weird."

"Like, weird about what," Sue questioned.

"That's kind of what I'm leading up to. I was wondering if– "

There is a click on the line as Mr. Andrews picked up the phone extension in his office. "Sue, are you almost done with the phone?"

"Daddy, I'll be off soon."

"Okay, but I need to call California in five minutes. There's a conference call about the contract and I have to be on the call on time. So, wrap it up."

"Okay, Daddy. I'll be off in four minutes. Sheeesh." Sue stomped her foot lightly on the floor as her frustration began to build. She wanted to know just what it was that Kirby was going to ask her and all of these delays were annoying her.

Click Mr. Andrews hung up the phone and left the two to talk alone.

"I can let you go if–," Kirby said before getting cut off abruptly by Sue.

"No, it's cool. What did you have to ask me?"

"Okay. This is kind of embarrassing, but I was wondering if– well, if you could ask Monika if she likes me? I'm kind of new to all of this, but I thought I felt sparks."

-- Silence –

"Sue, are you there," Kirby asked. He was nervous that he had said the wrong thing and that just maybe she had hung up on him.

"Um, yeah Kirby--I– "

"Sue--I have to use the phone now. You can use it when I'm done. Please hang up now," said Mr. Andrews.

"Sorry, Mr. Andrews it's me Kirby. I'll–I'll just call back later."

"Hey Kirb. Thanks pal. I need to talk to the record company about the contract. Business stuff, but you can call back in about an hour. Thanks buddy. I appreciate it."

"Okay. Sorry. Sue, I'll give you a call later."

"Um, yeah –"

Sue's Bear

Sue paced back and forth in her room. "What am I going to say to him?" She thought to herself. "I can't tell him that Monika thinks he's a dork, but I also can't lie to him and let him believe that she might like him. Arg!"

Frustrated, she ran over and jumped onto her bed. She buried her face in the pillows. "Mom would know what to do. She always had the answers–" Sue began to cry softly as tears flowed from her eyes and dampened the pillow case. She felt around with her hand until she felt the soft, spongy touch of her teddy bear. It was the same bear that she had won at the carnival a few summers ago. The whole family had gone together. The three of them had sat down at the game where you had to squirt water into the clown's mouth as a balloon over its head filled with air. The winner was the first person whose balloon popped. The game had been about to begin. Sue had raised her water gun and aimed it at the clowns open mouth. She looked briefly to her left and saw her Dad winking at her Mom who was on her right. Sue got a warm feeling in her heart. She was always so happy that her family was so loving in regards to each other. Her Mom and Dad loved each other and nothing could ever take that away. The bell rang and signaled the start of the game; the water guns came to life. Water squirted forward in an arcing stream into the clown's mouth. Sue's balloon was getting bigger and bigger. Just as it appeared as though it was going to pop she felt the cold rush of water as it sprayed on both sides of her head. She screamed just as her balloon popped. "We have a winner," exclaimed the man working the game as he handed Sue a medium brown teddy bear. Her parents laughed at the sight of Sue, her hair soaked and dripping, as she held her new stuffed animal tight to her chest. On the ride home from the carnival that night Sue heard her Dad laugh quietly to himself as she drifted off to sleep with the bear still in her arms.

Now as Sue lay on her bed she once again held that bear tightly to her chest as she sobbed large crocodile tears and drifted off to sleep.

Sue was awakened by the loud knocking on her door.

"Hey, Susie-Q," her Dad yelled out. "I'm done with the

phone."

There was silence as Sue's face remained planted on the bed. She still clutched her bear as she gathered her thoughts. The short nap had done nothing to ease the hurt and confusion that she felt.

"Susie, are you in there? Can I come in?--Sue? I'm coming in--here I come." He opened the door slowly and peered in. He saw her on the bed and heard her faint sobs. "Sue, what's wrong, honey? Why are you crying?"

Sue lifted her head and looked at her Dad. He saw the wet tracks of tears on her cheeks.

"It's all right, baby girl." He said as he sat on the edge of the bed and put an arm around her. "It's all right. Tell me what's wrong."

Through the sobs and sniffles Sue randomly spurted bits of information. "It's Mom--and Kirby--and I miss her. She'd know what to do."

"Yeah, I miss Mom too; a lot. She always did have a way of knowing just what to do. Is it anything I can help with?"

Sue sat up and dried her eyes on a nearby stuffed unicorn then put both the unicorn and her bear back on her pillow. "It's Kirby. He called today and had this big question for me."

"What did he ask you?"

"He--he wanted me to ask Monika if she likes him and I don't know what to do. She thinks he's a dork, but he feels so good about himself. I don't want to crush his spirits."

"That's nice of you to think of him. Is that the only reason? Do you like Kirby at all?"

"Daddy!"

"Well?"

"No--I mean--we had a good time the other day when he was here. You were right. I gave him a chance and he is a really fun and nice person to hang out with. But that was one day. He's nice, but--I don't know."

"Susie, you've got to do what's right. If he's a friend then he deserves the truth. I would tell him that it's not a great idea right now. He doesn't have to know exactly what she thinks."

"I guess. I dunno–"

"Hey! I forgot to tell you! I have big news! The record company wants me to come out to California this coming weekend.

They want to have a face-to-face meeting with me to talk more about the contract. Isn't that great?"

"That's awesome, Daddy!"

"Dry those tears. Let's go celebrate! Let's have a big dinner! You choose where we go!"

"Okay. Let me call Kirby quick and tell him that I'll call him back later. I think that will give me some time to think about what I should tell him."

You're Jealous

"Well, that was a pretty good dinner." Sue's dad said as he opened the front door of the house and walked in.

"Yeah. It was great," Sue replied. "I can't believe how many of those ribs you ate."

"It was an All You Can Eat buffet. If they're going to put the meat out then I am going to eat it!" Ron Andrews laughed and rubbed his stomach with his hands. "That was so good." There was a long pause as he thought about what to say next or if he should mention anything at all. Against his better judgment he decided to ask Sue about the Kirby situation. He felt that is what her mother would have done. "So, going to call Kirby now? Do you have any idea what you're going to tell him?"

Sue paused and thought for a moment before she answered. "Well, I think that you're right. I think that I have to tell him the truth."

"Let him down easy, Sue," he said patting her lightly on the shoulder. "This will probably be his first broken heart, so try to let him down easy."

"I'll try, Daddy."

Sue went into the den and sat down at the computer. She checked her email and then, in her head, she began to practice the lines that she was going to say to Kirby. She thought of the nicest words that would get the point across, but not crush his heart. When she had just the right words she picked up the phone and called Kirby.

The phone rang twice in her ear before a woman's voice said, "Hello?"

"Hi, this is Sue. Is Kirby there?" Sue's palms began to sweat. This was not a call that she really wanted to make, but she felt that is what a friend would do and she wanted to do what was right.

"Oh, hi Sue he's in his room. Let me get him," said Kirby's mom. There was a quiet clunk as she set the phone on the counter and called out to Kirby.

There is another clunking sound as Kirby picked up the phone. "Hey, Susie-Q how was dinner?"

"Hey Kirby. It was good," Sue said. Her voice began to trail off and fade out, but in all his excitement Kirby didn't even notice.

"Cool. So, did you get a chance to call Monika yet?"

"Uh, well, not exactly. We took off right after I called you earlier and we just got home a few minutes ago. But, um, I did want to talk to you about that." Sue swallowed hard as the words she had planned on saying became jumbled in her head.

"Okay, cool. So, how ya gonna do it? Just call her and ask her or maybe wait until we're in school tomorrow and ask her at her locker or at one of your campaign meetings? I'm not sure how this all works, but I am very psyched about the whole thing."

"Well, to be honest–," Sue sighed. "Um, I don't think that now is the right time for this. I mean, like, she's Monika. She's-- well, she's my friend, but, you know, sometimes she can be a handful. I'm just not sure that it's a good idea right now."

"What do you mean? Did she say something?" Kirby asked.

"No. It's--you know–she's got the campaign for school President and–I, I dunno--maybe she's not your type."

"What do you mean not my type? What are you trying to say? I felt something. We had a moment. She invited me to her house this weekend." Kirby began to get angry.

"Kirby, as a friend I'm just trying to tell you that she's just being nice to you to get your vote," Sue reluctantly said.

"You're just saying that. We had a moment and it was nice. You -- you're jealous!"

"What?!?!" Sue almost dropped the phone when she heard Kirby say that she was jealous.

"I think that maybe you're jealous because she likes me."

"Kirby, it's not like that. You're a good guy and I just don't think that Monika is right for you."

"You're jealous! I know you are! Why else would you say stuff like this?"

"Kirby! She said you're a dork! She said you were a dork the minute you walked away from the table. D! O! R! K! DORK!"

"That's a lie and you know it! We had a moment! She likes me and for whatever reason, you are jealous! I don't need you! I'll ask her myself tomorrow!"

"Kirby, don't– "

CLICK

Kirby hung up the phone and ran into his bedroom. He slammed the door behind him and dove onto his bed.

Sue sat and listened to the monotonous drone of the dial tone in her ear.

After a few minutes Sue hung up the phone. All of her feelings came rushing head-on into her brain. She jumped up from the chair and ran quickly up the stairs. She brushed by her Dad as she turned and bolted for her bedroom.

"Hey, where's the fire?" He asked.

Remembering Mom

Sue stood in her doorway and yelled out, "This is all your fault! I told Kirby the truth and he hung up on me. Now he's going to ask Monika out tomorrow and he hates me. This is all YOUR fault! I wish Mom were here!" Then she turned and slammed the door shut.

From out in the hallway, Ron Andrews could hear the muffled sounds of Sue as she began to cry for the second time that day. Thinking that it was best to give her some space, he turned and headed downstairs.

Inside her room, Sue cried a river of tears. She was mad and sad and missed her mom. She hugged her stuffed teddy bear tightly while she rocked back and forth. She thought about Kirby and Monika and wondered why life wasn't fair.

About an hour passed when she heard a light knock at the door. At that point Sue was all cried out and was sitting on the end of her bed as she stared out the window. "Come in," she said quietly.

The door slowly opened and in walked her dad. Without saying a word he came in and sat down next to her on the bed. With one hand he stroked her long brown hair.

"You know, your hair is just like Mom's when I first met her; long and straight. That was how she always wore it back when we were dating."

"Yeah," Sue said. Her gaze was still focused outside the window fixated on nothing specific; she just looked out and beyond her room. She thought of how things would be different if her Mom were still with them.

"One time, before you were born, we went on a cruise to the Caribbean. At every island we stopped the locals would ask her if she wanted her hair braided. Politely, she'd tell them no. We'd get twenty feet away and another person would ask her again. This happened wherever we went. Finally, at the last island, I think it was St. Maarten she gave in and let this one old woman braid it. The woman told us stories of the island while she worked on Mom's hair. She braided every last strand nice and neat. She even worked in some colorful beads."

"It sounds kind of nice," Sue said as she pulled at her own hair and imagined in her head what she would look like with braids and beads in her hair.

"It was--or at least I thought so. We walked around the market place and with every step that she took the beads clicked and clacked together. The constant noise drove your mom crazy! Then when we got back to our cabin on the ship and she saw herself in the mirror she just about flipped. She hated it!" He laughed out. "'*You said it looked nice*' she yelled out at me. She started to try and pick out the braids, but the old island woman had braided it so tight that she couldn't do it. Oh boy, she was furious with me!"

"Holy cow! What did she do?"

"Well, we spent one day at sea before returning to port and then flying home. The very next day after we returned home she went to a beautician, but not her regular one. She had to go somewhere where they didn't know her and she had them cut out the braids. When I first saw it I had to hide the look of shock on my face. Her hair was so incredibly short that I didn't really recognize her at first."

"No way!"

"Oh yeah! She came home with her short hair and spent the rest of the night crying on the bed. For almost a week she wouldn't go outside."

"What happened after that," Sue asked.

"Well, finally it started to grow longer and longer until it was all back. It was long and brown just like yours."

"Sometimes I miss her so much, Daddy. It's just not fair."

"I know, honey," he said and hugged her tight. "But she's up there watching us now and she knows we're trying. You know I try, right? I do my best, but I know I'm not Mom. I really thought that it was best to tell Kirby the truth," Mr. Andrews explained. "I thought that was the best way to go."

"I guess it was, but he got all crazy and said that I was jealous. And I'm not--really. He's nice, but--I dunno. I just don't want Monika to hurt him and I know that she'd just use him for a vote."

"That's all that matters. You tried to help him. It will all work out. Trust me."

Sue looked over at her dad and smiled. "I sure hope that somehow it does work out."

The next day at school Sue saw Kirby immediately as she entered the hallway. He was leaned up against the lockers with his back to her. She quickened her pace as she moved toward him. She wanted to talk to him and to set things straight between the two of them – and maybe apologize if she had hurt him.

As she neared him she saw Monika on the far side of Kirby. There was a small gap between the locker and Kirby. Monika glared through this gap at Sue. Sue stopped dead in her tracks and stood in the middle of the hallway not sure what to do next.

"OK, cool. So we're still on for this weekend, right?" Monika said.

"Sure thing!" Kirby replied.

"It sounds great to me. I'll talk to you later." Monika said as she gave him a long semi-passionate look before she turned and walked away.

Kirby turned around with a big smile on his face and watched her walk away. He saw Sue standing in the hallway. "Oh, hey, Sue."

"Hey, Kirby. Look, about last night. I just wanted to say– "

"No need to say anything. I talked to Monika and come to find out, you were right. She's so wrapped up with this campaign that she doesn't really have time for a boyfriend right now. She did say that maybe I could still come over this weekend to help her with her computer."

"That's good I guess," Sue replied somewhat confused.

"One thing though. I asked her about calling me a dork. I mean, if we have any shot of doing this long term then I figured that now was the best time to get it out in the open. She denied it at first, but then said that she caved in to the peer pressure. She said that Janie was the one that called me a dork and she said that she was sorry for agreeing with her because clearly I'm not a dork at all. She said that she thought that you said it too, but wasn't sure."

Sue's jaw dropped open. "Uh, well, I–"

"Sue, don't worry about it. The old Kirby got called names all of the time. I'm used to it, but I think it's a thing of the past. Once I'm dating Monika everyone will see that I'm not a dork. I mean, I'm being kind of premature with this, but she did say that she'd think about it when her schedule opened up a bit after the campaign. So, that's kind of cool."

"Yeah, that's--uh--something."

Just Not My Day

Later that day

"Sue. I need to talk to you."

It's Monika and the tone in her voice was not a happy one. As always, Janie was tagging along right behind her.

"Sue, we really need to talk," Monika said as she stood in front of Sue with her hands on her hips and a serious look on her face.

"Sure, Mon I've got a couple of great ideas for the campaign."

"Well, don't worry about it. Janie is going to be handling my campaign from now on."

Janie nodded in agreement. "That's right. We're going to win this thing."

"Oh," Sue said as a wave of shock slowly rolled over her.

"Yeah, she's a lot more focused than you are and isn't all boy crazy over some dork. Oh and she's not plotting behind my back."

"What are you talking about," Sue questioned. "I--"

Monika walked up close to Sue. Sue slowly stepped backwards until she felt the cold cement wall come up behind her. Monika was right in her face.

"Look, I don't know what you told Kirby about me and, to be honest, I really don't care. If you ruin this campaign any further for me I will ruin you and your family. My dad knows a lot of people--a lot of people in the entertainment industry. I heard that your Dad is trying to get a new recording contract. If I lose this campaign I will personally see to it that he never earns another dime. You, your dad, and that loser Kirby can all live on food stamps!"

"Yeah," Janie added, "Food stamps!"

Monika glared at Sue one more time then turned and walked away with Janie in tow.

Sue's knees got weaker and weaker until they gave way and her body slid slowly down the wall into a sitting position. With her backpack slumped alongside her, Sue put her head into her hands in frustration.

"This just hasn't been my day," she muttered quietly to no one. "Not my day at all."

The Big Meeting

"Hey, Dad? Are you in here?" Sue yelled out as she walked into her dad's bedroom. Clothes were scattered all over the bed and the floor.

"Yeah Susie-Q, I'm just packing some things for my trip to Cali. I can't figure out which shirt to pack for my big meeting. Maybe the black one with the silver stripes or the plain off-white one, or maybe the—"

Sue interrupted, "Dad, you should sit down for this."

He looked at her and was very puzzled. Even though he was in a rush to get his things packed for his trip he made room on the edge of the bed for the both of them and sat down. He patted the open spot next to him and said, "Sit down. Now what's on your mind?"

"Dad, I have something very important to tell you, but I don't want you to flip out or anything when I tell you what I have to tell you."

"Okay." His heart raced at the thought of what his teenage daughter had to tell him that was so serious. It was moments like this that Ron Andrews dreaded the most about being a single father.

"Promise me, Daddy. You have to *not* flip out," she insisted.

"Uh, okay. I promise not to completely flip out now. Can I flip out later," he joked.

"Daddy! Seriously! This is important."

"Okay, I promise. Now tell me. What is so important?"

Sue Andrews looked over at her father and took a deep breath. "Dad, today at school I had a little run in with Monika and besides firing me as her campaign manager, she also said that she'd ruin your music career. Don't worry though. I handled it and everything will be okay."

"What? What are you talking about, Sue?"

"She said that if I mess up the campaign for her that she will ruin your music career. She said that her dad knows a lot of important people and–"

"Let me cut you off there," he said as he held in the laughter, but still grinned uncontrollably from ear to ear. "Sue, Monika's dad may be rich and he might drive a fancy car and wear fancy suits out to

69

dinner, but he's only a dentist."

Sue stood and looked puzzled. She didn't understand. She had just told her dad that this man was going to crush his career and he acted as if he didn't have a care in the world.

"He's just a dentist. He knows other dentists and maybe a handful of doctors--and from what I heard some nurses as well. I'm not sure what world Monika lives in, but this isn't the 90210 zip code. Tell her to cut the drama. You don't be so worried about what she thinks her dad can do." Ron Andrews could not restrain himself any longer and began to laugh very loud and shook his head. "He's a dentist, Sue; only a dentist."

"Well, that is a relief." Sue exhaled and felt the weight of this important news being lifted from her shoulders.

"So what's this about her kicking you off of the campaign?"

"Kirby and she were talking and–"

"Susie, let me cut you off again. You don't have to explain. I gotta tell ya something. It might be difficult to understand now, but you don't need friends like Monika. It seems like she has a hidden agenda for everything. If you ask me, she is a little insecure and very immature for her age. Find some good friends and don't worry about Kirby. He'll understand that she's all smoke and mirrors soon enough. If you're his friend, you'll be there to help pick up the pieces."

"I guess. So, anyway while you're gone I'll have nothing to do really. I guess just hang out with Aunt Elizabeth," Sue said with a sigh as she thought about how bored that she will be while her aunt is around.

"Ah, it's not that bad and it's only for the weekend."

"Daddy, I know she is your sister, but she treats me like I'm in boot camp and she is the Drill Sergeant. I mean, she makes me say "Yes Ma'am" when I talk to her. Who does that?"

"It'll be fine. Plus, you're not really old enough to stay alone for the entire weekend. She'll be here at night, but you'll have your days to yourself. She'll be calling to check in on you, but this will give you some alone time. And I mean ALONE time! No visitors while I'm gone!"

"I'd first need some friends before I had visitors," Sue laughed.

"You know what I mean," he said. "Now help me pick out the right suit to wear for this meeting. It has to be sharp, but with a little edge to it. I want to show those Record Execs that Ron Andrews is still rad!"

Sue rolls her eyes. "I'll try, Daddy, but I'm not a magician."

Kirby Meets Aunt Elizabeth

Saturday Afternoon

RING -- RING – RING

"Hello?" Sue said as she picked up the phone.

"Hey, Sue! This is Kirby. What's up?" He sounded happy and full of energy.

"Uh, not much I guess. I haven't heard from you much lately. Where ya been?"

"Well, just kind of doin' my thing, ya know," said Kirby.

"I thought that you were going to Monika's house today to do something with her computer," Sue asked with a hint of jealousy in her voice. "I mean doesn't she have some major computer problem that only you can fix?"

"She did and I was, but at the last minute she had to go do something with a sick aunt of hers, so she gave me a rain check on it," Kirby said as he sat on the couch and stuck his finger through a hole in one of his socks. "I thought I'd give you a call and see what's up."

"Oh," Sue said and tried to hold back her laughter "*Sure, a sick aunt. I bet,*" she said to herself. "*That's the best you could come up with, Monika?*"

"Sue? Are you there," Kirby asked.

"Um, uh, yeah. I just uh—"

"Anyway," Kirby interrupted. "I figured that since we haven't done much with the project lately that maybe I could come over and we could work on it."

"I don't know. My dad is in California and he said that I'm not supposed to have anyone over. My Aunt Elizabeth is here at night with me. She's not here now, but she'll be here later. Maybe I can ask her then."

"I guess. I mean, it's just school work, but whatever. Monika said that–"

"Monika said WHAT?" Sue could only imagine what lies Monika had been planting in Kirby's head.

"Well, Monika said that you might act this way. You know, jealous and all."

"Kirby, are you serious? You know what? Forget it. Come over whenever you want to. I don't care! I really don't care," Sue said as she hung up the phone with a loud *CLICK*.

Kirby hung up the phone and walked into his bedroom. He took out the binder of research information for the project and put on his NY Yankees windbreaker. As he was about to leave he thought about the hole in his sock and quickly put on a pair fresh pair that had no holes. He quickly called his mom who was at work to let her know that he was going over to Sue's house to study. He walked down to the Bus Stop and caught the next bus headed in the direction of Sue's house.

KNOCK KNOCK KNOCK

Sue was surprised by the loud and unexpected knock at the front door. She grabbed the phone and dialed 9-1, then looked out the curtains and was prepared to dial the final 1 if she saw an intruder on the steps. She hung up the phone when she saw Kirby standing there with the research binder tucked under his right elbow.

"Hey, Kirby," She said as she opened the front door.

"Hi. Can I come in?" Kirby asked with a big smile on his face. He extended the research binder out in her direction. "I brought the binder so that we can get some work done on our project," he explained.

Sue hesitated and then reluctantly said, "Okay, you can come in but you can't stay for long." Sue looked out into the street to make sure that no one was watching and then quickly shut the door behind Kirby as he walked inside.

Confused by Sue's actions, Kirby asked, "I thought you said I could come over so we could work on the project?"

"Yeah, I--well--I did, but you have to leave before my aunt gets here."

"Okay," Kirby said and shrugged his shoulders. "Let's get to work then."

Sue led him into the den and pulled a second chair over to the computer desk. Kirby sat down and immediately began to type on the computer.

"What are you doing?" Sue asked somewhat confused.

"I just wanted to log in to my Google Talk account and see if Janie had heard anything about Monika."

"Kirby, did you come here to work or to–"

"That's weird. It shows that Monika is logged in."

'Hey U. How R things? How R U? Is UR aunt OK?' Kirby typed and then tapped the ENTER key.

After few seconds he saw both Monika and Janie's profile go grey signifying that they have both logged off.

"That was weird. I hope she's okay. Maybe I should call her."

"Look, Kirby. Let's try to do some research here. I mean isn't that why you came over anyway?"

"But maybe she needs a shoulder to cry on or just someone to listen in her time of need."

"Holy crap! Are you hearing yourself? Kirby, look, I want to be your friend. I like you, but you really need to open your eyes and realize what Monika is doing. And before you say it--I am not jealous. SO get that thought out of your head right now. She treats you like crap, but you're blind to it because you like her and you think that she likes you. But Kirby--as a friend, I'm telling you--I've been friends with Monika for a while and I'm pretty sure that she doesn't even have an aunt. She has two uncles. One is single and the other is gay. She doesn't have an aunt, let alone one that is sick. Please listen to me for once. Please," Sue said. As soon as the words had left her mouth she wished that she could have taken them back. She felt mean and rude and awkward all at the same time. Her feet began to tangle around each other as her eyes drifted to the floor. She couldn't look Kirby in the eye right at that moment.

"Wow. I uh--I guess--wow! I don't know what to say. Is she that bad of a person? I mean, why would she do this?" He said sad, shocked, and dejected.

"Kirby, I don't know why she does what she does. My dad says that she is insecure, but sometimes I think she is just evil. I'm not going to tell you what to do, but please be careful." Sue felt better about telling Kirby to be careful. She felt that is what a friend would do. She brought her gaze up from the floor and looked Kirby in the eyes again. "That's all I wanted to say. Just be careful."

"I don't know what to say, Sue." Kirby said staring deep into her eyes. "I…" Kirby tilted his head and slowly leaned into Sue. His lips puckered as he neared her face.

"SUSAN ALICE ANDREWS! What in the Sam Hill are you doing?"

Aunt Elizabeth stood with her hands on her hips and glared at both Sue and Kirby. She was not too happy with the situation that she had walked in on.

More Big News

Late Sunday Night

The front door opened and in walked Sue's dad. He had returned home from his trip to California. He stood just inside the door with a suitcase in one hand and a huge box in the other.

"Susie-Q!" He yelled out.

Aunt Elizabeth came in from the kitchen. "Good evening, Ronald. I hope that your flight was enjoyable and that your trip was beneficial to your career."

Ron Andrews stared at his sister as if she were an alien.

"Um, yeah. It was a good trip. Where's my Susie tonight?" He asked.

"She's up in her room," Elizabeth replied.

"Great. Go get her please while I set these things down. I have some great news for everyone."

Elizabeth walked upstairs and shouted from the hallway outside of Sue's bedroom. "Susan. Come down stairs."

From inside her room she muttered, "Yes, Ma'am. Be right there, Ma'am."

Slowly Sue's door opened and she trotted down the stairs. "Daddy, I didn't know that you were home!" She exclaimed as she ran over and launched herself into his outstretched arms. He hugged her tightly. "How was the trip? Did you see any movie stars? Did you get me anything?"

"Whoa, slow down," he laughed. "I didn't see any movie stars, but I did get you a nice little gift. It's over there in that box, but before you open it I have great news! Let's go into the living room. You're going to want to be sitting down when you hear this."

The three of them walked into the living room. Aunt Elizabeth and Sue sat at opposite ends of the couch.

"Well. Oh man! I don't even know where to start. Okay. So I met with some of the record execs and they had me record some basic vocal tracks. I guess it was just to see if I still had the pipes or not. But they loved what they heard. They loved it so much that they want me to do an entire new CD that also includes a remake of The Ronster

Romp. They think it can be updated and that this generation will just dig it!"

"That's so awesome daddy," Sue exclaimed.

"Yes. Ronald. That is very nice," Elizabeth said.

"Oh, it gets better. It's a two record contract! They want to sign me to a two record contract with a big pay day!"

"HOLY Cow Daddy! This is amazing! You're going to be more popular than Clay Aiken," Sue said jumping up and down in her excitement.

"Okay. I don't know what that means, but if this record takes off I will be more popular than maybe even Cassius Clay!"

"I'm happy for you, Ronald," Elizabeth added.

"There's one more thing to make it even better," Mr. Andrews said.

"Yes, Daddy what is it? What more could there be?" Sue questioned and stood on her tip-toes in anticipation.

"Well, the record company is putting us up in a nice house in the hills. We're moving to Los Angeles!" He proclaimed.

This news hit Sue like a ton of bricks. Her knees weaken and she slumped further into the couch. She took several deep breaths, but couldn't seem to catch her breath.

"Ronald. I think that you've hyperventilated the girl. Do something."

Mr. Andrews looked at Elizabeth again and ran over to Sue's side. "Are you okay, honey? Want some water? Liz, do something useful and go get her a glass of water."

Sue looked up at him with tears in her eyes. "I don't want to move," she stuttered through the sobs. "This is our house. Why can't you record from here?"

"Sue," he said as he ran his hand on her back and tried to comfort her. "That's just the way the business works. You'll make some new friends in California and everything will be fine. Plus, once the record is done and the tour is over, we can do all kinds of fun stuff."

"A tour?" She mumbled.

"A tour? Ronald, a tour is no place for a young girl." Elizabeth commented.

"Don't worry. We'll work out the details. But this is good news, Susie. We're going to have lots of nice stuff and live a new life. Trust me, you'll get used to it."

"I guess." She said and sobbed a little more. "I guess."

Later that evening after Aunt Elizabeth left and Mr. Andrews unpacked his suitcases.

"Knock, knock. Sue, can I come in?" Her dad said from just outside of her slightly opened bedroom door.

"Sure Dad. I was just getting ready to go to bed."

"I need to talk to you before you do. Look, Aunt Liz told me that Kirby was here. She said that she caught you guys in the throes of passion. Is this true?" This was another one of the moments that Ron Andrews had always feared and wished deeply that his wife were here to deal with his daughter.

"I know he wasn't supposed to be here, but he was being a jerk on the phone about Monika. She blew him off and so he called me to come over and study. I told him no at first, but he said that Monika said that I would say that because I was just jealous. To prove I wasn't jealous I kind of sort of said that he could come over--but it was only to study. Once he got here all he did was say 'Monika this and Monika that'. I got really sick of it and told him just what type of person Monika really is and told him to do what he wanted. I also told him that I was his friend and I would be here no matter what. I guess it sank in and he was speechless. That's when I guess he was leaning in to kiss me and that's when Aunt Elizabeth snuck in on us. But nothing happened. He left right after that and she grounded me for the rest of the weekend."

"Well, you know that I didn't want anyone over here at all. No one was supposed to be here, not even Kirby. And she didn't sneak up on you. She walked into the house where she was supposed to be. She was right to ground you and I think you're going to be grounded for the next two weeks on top of that. You're right home after school and no internet and no TV."

"OK. I'm sorry, Daddy, but that Monika makes me so mad sometimes that I lose my mind!"

"It's okay. Go to sleep now. I'll see you in the morning." He said and kissed her lightly on the forehead.

Who To Vote For?

The Next Day at School

Sue was standing next to her locker talking to Kirby. "--yeah, and then he said that I was grounded for the next two weeks."

"Sorry. I didn't mean to get you in trouble," Kirby said.

"It's okay. At least this will give me the time I need to really buckle down on this project." Sue rolled her eyes and wished for the next two weeks to pass as fast as possible.

"Yeah, by the way, the elections are this Wednesday. Do you know who you're going to vote for?" Kirby asked.

"I'm not sure," Sue said. "I might not even vote."

"Seriously? You should vote for Monika. I know things are weird between you guys, but she's basically running on all of the ideas that you gave her when you were helping her. It's like you're the one who got her this far."

"Yeah. Thanks for reminding me," Sue said as she hit Kirby playfully in the arm. "I think I'll be voting for Myron Albertson-- if I vote at all."

"Well, well, well, if it isn't the two biggest losers whacking each other in the hallway," Monika said as she walked up from behind them. "Sue, I don't want to even talk to you and Kirby, you dear have betrayed me for the last time. I know you were over at her house while I was worried sick about my auntie."

Kirby grinned and looked at Sue.

"What? What was that grin for?" Monika shouted. Some of the other kids in the hallway looked in their direction. "Let me guess, Little Miss Nothing told you that I don't have an aunt, right? Well screw you both. I don't need your votes. As per Janie's figures I have this election wrapped up. Isn't that right, Janie?"

Janie nodded in agreement.

Kirby and Sue both looked at each other and began to shout out loud, "MYRON! MYRON! VOTE FOR MYRON!"

Monika glared at the two of them and stormed away down the hallway.

Sue and Kirby high-fived each other and laughed. "It would serve her right if Myron won," Kirby said.

"It sure would," said Sue as she winked at Kirby. "It sure would."

And The Winner Is...

Wednesday at School

"Okay class. Attention please," said Mr. Walton as he looked around the classroom; always on the lookout for notes being passed and secrets being whispered. "In about five minutes we will be lining up and going to the gymnasium where Principal Heffernan will announce the results of the school election today. Please be on your best behavior."

"You voted for Myron, right?" Kirby whispered to Sue.

Sue nodded her head slightly up and down. "Yes," she mouthed silently to him.

Kirby winked at her. "I think a lot of people did!" He said.

"Mr. Carson, is there something you would like to share with the class?" Mr. Walton asked.

Kirby replied, "No, Sir." He felt his face get red.

"Then please be quiet." Mr. Walton looked up at the clock that hung above the doorway. "Okay, class line up outside in the hallway. It's time to go to the gymnasium."

The class rose to their feet and slowly filed out into the hallway where they lined up single file against the wall. As soon as Mr. Walton gave the signal the class began to walk. Quickly the single file formation broke down and the students all walked in little groups. Random words could be heard emanating from the buzz of the students chatter. "Myron," said one girl. "Monika," said another. "Henry," said some kid with a missing tooth and a black eye.

"Class please quiet down." Mr. Walton said, but it was no use; the excitement of the class election had put a charge into the students and getting them to quiet down was a losing battle.

As the students entered the gymnasium the quiet buzz increased to a dull roar. The rest of the school was there and most were already seated. Mr. Walton's class sat in empty spots near the front of the bleachers as Principal Heffernan walked up onto the stage and to the microphone on the podium. A paper airplane floated lazily through the air to the right of the stage.

"Please settle down," Principal Heffernan said.

SCREEEEEEEECH. The sound of feedback filled the room. Principal Heffernan looked oddly at the microphone and then lowered it away from his mouth until the noise had stopped. "Okay everyone. Welcome. Today we are gathered to announce the results from the class election. Seated behind me are the candidates representing all of the positions for which you have voted. I want to congratulate the winners and thank everyone for an exciting election. So now, here are your results. The new Class Treasurer is--"

"Kirby. Pssst. Kirby. I talked to some people on the way down here. Pam said that someone was saying that last night Monika kicked Janie off of her campaign team. Tommy said that he heard that Janie voted for Myron!" Sue whispered to Kirby. All around them the crowd of students applauded the winners as Principal Heffernan announced the results of the different races.

"That's crazy!" Kirby replied.

"Finally I'd like to announce the results for the position of Class President. This was the closest race out of them all. I personally want to thank both candidates, Myron Albertson and Monika Randolph, for running a fair and honest race. Please give a round of applause for both of these fine people." A smattering of cheers and claps echoed through the gymnasium. "The winner, receiving 62 percent of the votes is…Myron Albertson!"

The crowd of students erupted in a thunderous applause as Myron rose from his chair and faced Monika who was still seated to his right. He extended his hand in her direction. Monika looked at him and stood up. She looked out at the cheering crowd and ran quickly from the stage. As she ran past the bleachers she spotted Sue in the crowd. Monika paused in front of the bleachers where Sue was seated. "You did this!" She mouthed as tears began to form in her eyes. "This is all your fault!" Then Monika disappeared into the crowd and out the door into the hallway.

Sue and Kirby looked at each other with shock and disbelief; both had small grins on their faces.

"Okay. Well, I guess that concludes today's assembly," said Principal Heffernan, "Please return calmly to your classrooms."

Mr. Walton gathered his class and herded them back to the classroom as orderly as possible. Although, he knew that any lesson taught today would be overshadowed by the events of this morning.

Later that day after school Sue ran into Kirby as he was about to get on his bus.

"Wanna come over to my house and work on this project? It's due next week you know," Sue said.

"Is your Dad cool with that?" Kirby asked.

"Yeah, he kind of mellowed out about the whole thing. Plus, I wanted to talk to you about something."

Kirby turned a slight shade of red. "What? What did you want to talk about?"

The Walk Home

Quietly, Sue and Kirby walked back into the school and down the hall to the pay phone near the nurse's office. First, Kirby called his mom to let her know that he was headed over to Sue's house. Sue then called her dad to let him know that they were going to walk home from school. Mr. Andrews gave Sue a hard time and insisted on coming to pick them up, but finally he gave in when Sue told him in a whisper that she needed to talk to Kirby about some important stuff.

Once they got outside the two friends began to walk in the direction of Sue's house. Sue was looking around at a flock of birds that were flying from tree to tree. She was amused at their indecision to pick one spot to sit and rest. For a brief moment Kirby wondered if fate would play a cruel trick on him and half expected Henry Martin to show up to ruin his alone time with Sue. "*The old Kirby thought like that,*" he said to himself. Kirby saw an old tennis ball near the curb and began to kick at it with his feet as they continued to walk. Both of them remained quiet for some time until Kirby finally broke the silence.

Although he was almost afraid of the answer he had a burning question that he just had to ask Sue. "Do I dare ask what it was that you wanted to talk to me about?" He blurted out.

Sue, somewhat startled by the mild outburst, was relieved that Kirby had broken the silence

"Well, there's no easy way of saying this so I'm just going to come out and say it. Remember the last time you were at my house and my Aunt Elizabeth walked into the room?"

"You don't have to remind me. I was embarrassed and scared. I've never run out of anywhere so fast in my life!"

"Well, you were about to do something. I mean, it almost looked like you were going to--going to kiss me."

"I, um, well, I...if...I – wellllllllllll," Kirby stammered and stuttered unable to make any sense. He lost control of the tennis ball that he had been kicking along. It bounced away from him, rolled into the street, and in the direction of a gutter. A small brown dog ran out from a nearby porch and snatched the tennis ball before it reached the gutter and then ran away behind the house with the ball firmly in his mouth.

"Kirby, I told you that day that I was your friend and I told you that I liked you. I do like you and, well, I would have liked that kiss from you." Sue stopped walking and turned to face Kirby.

Kirby stopped walking and wasn't sure what to do. First he looked at his shoes, and then at the dog running around in the backyard playing with the tennis ball, and then he looked at Sue. "I, um, well--yeah--it--welllll--"

"Here, let me help you find the words," Sue said as she leaned in closer to him and placed her lips on his. She gave him the world's softest first kiss ever.

Shocks of electricity seemed to shoot from her lips and stunned Kirby. He stood motionless as Sue looked at him, grinned, and began to slowly walk away. "Hey, um wait up!" He finally said. "What, what was that for?"

"I like you. That's all. You're a nice person and I wanted you to know that."

"Well, does this mean that you are my girlfriend?"

"I guess. If you want to call it that," She said with a big smile.

"Woo hoo!" Kirby yelled at the top of his lungs. "Hey! Bird in the sky! This is my girlfriend! Hey fire hydrant! Meet my girlfriend, Sue!"

"You're such a dork!" She said playfully.

"I am!" Kirby said and ran in crazy circles up and down the sidewalk until he abruptly stopped.

"What's up?" Sue said.

"Well, it just occurred to me. You're moving in three weeks. This is just my luck!" Kirby said as he kicked at the ground below his feet. "I finally get my first girlfriend and she is moving 2000 miles away! Arg!"

"It's okay, Kirby. We'll have the best three weeks ever," Sue said as she took Kirby's hand in hers.

"I guess," he said as he looked down at his hand as it sat firmly in the hand of his first ever real girlfriend. He looked up at Sue and smiled. "I've got a girlfriend," he whispered to her.

They continued to walk and talk and laugh and hold hands as they made their way to Sue's house.

As they entered her house Sue's dad was in the living room.

He got up and walked into the kitchen. Sue was getting Kirby a bottle of soda from the refrigerator. "So, who won?" Mr. Andrews asked.

"MYRON!" Sue and Kirby both exclaimed in unison.

"Daddy, Monika was so mad! She stormed off of the stage and she was mad! She left school before we returned to class. No one saw her the rest of the day."

"Oh wow!" He replied.

"We're going to work on our project in the den," Sue said. "Come on, Kirby. We can download those pictures and print them out in the den."

The three of them walked into the den together. Kirby and Sue sat down at the computer desk while Mr. Andrews hovered nearby.

"So, how are things, Kirby?" Mr. Andrews asked, "Anything new?"

"I'm pretty good, Mr. Andrews, pretty good!" He said in a very chipper voice.

"Holy cow, you have got to see this! Monika emailed me and blamed me for her loss! This is too funny! She wrote that she is going to call her dad now and have him ruin your career Daddy! I wonder if her big dentist daddy is going to laugh in her face."

The three of them laughed as Mr. Andrews shook his head. "She'll get over it someday."

The Big Move

For the next two weeks Kirby and Sue spent a lot of time together. Every night after school they studied together; they split time between the library, Kirby's house and Sue's house. On the weekends they were taking in movies, going for bike rides, and one afternoon they even had a nice picnic in Sue's backyard. In school Kirby and Sue feverishly passed notes back and forth while all the time hoping that Mr. Walton wouldn't catch them and read the notes in front of the class.

When Mr. Andrews questioned Sue about all of the time that she was spending with Kirby, Sue reluctantly admitted that they were boyfriend and girlfriend. Mr. Andrews was in shock that his baby girl was old enough to date, although he did have an idea that something was up the day that Sue called and asked him if she could walk home with Kirby. He tried not to make a big deal of it, but still found time to kid Sue about her new boyfriend when the chance arose.

The first two weeks flew by all too fast for the young romantics and the last week was a hectic one for everyone.

Much to Sue's relief, Monika never returned to George Knipfing Middle School. Janie said that Monika had her father transfer her to a private school in Connecticut because she was more interested in developing herself for the future instead of wasting all of her time hanging around with losers. Janie also told them that she thinks that it was simply because Monika was embarrassed about losing to Myron and that people finally knew that she was full of lies.

Kirby and Sue finished their project for Mr. Walton's class and had given the presentation in front of everyone. Kirby, still somewhat shy, held on tightly to the podium while Sue did the majority of the talking. Afterward they both agreed that they worked very well together as a team. Their hard work and effort paid off and Mr. Walton gave them both a grade of A-.

Sue and her Dad began the huge task of boxing up all of their belongings in preparation for the big move. Kirby, of course, was there every day to help them. Slowly the house began to look bare. It looked less and less like a home and more like a storage facility. Large boxes filled the den and most of the living room. In the kitchen was a large stack of flat boxes. From time to time Kirby would run down the stairs and use the tape gun to assemble a few boxes and then shoot back upstairs where Sue would fill them with her stuffed animals, books, and keepsakes. That coming Saturday morning everything had to be ready so that the movers could load it all onto the truck.

Friday evening Mr. Andrews invited Kirby and his mom over for dinner. Kirby felt awkward having his mom over for dinner at his girlfriend's house, but he was more concerned about spending all of the time with Sue that he possibly could. That would be Sue's last night in town and Kirby wanted to make the best of it. It had been a long week of packing and everyone was ready to relax with a nice dinner. "It wouldn't be a special night with the Andrews' if we didn't make pizza!" Mr. Andrews proclaimed. "Kirby, you should be a pro at this now. Jump right up there and help your mom make a good one." Everyone laughed while they splashed sauce and sprinkled cheese on their dough. In fact, the entire night was filled with laughter and good times. A few times during the night Kirby would stand back and soak in the moment. He had an idea that this would be one of the best nights of his life and he wanted to remember every detail.

During dinner, Kirby's Mom admitted that she was a fan of The Ronster Romp back when it was originally released. "Well, I still have some records unpacked if you want to listen to some music?" Mr. Andrew's pulled out her chair and led her into the living room.

She looked at the kids and gave Mr. Andrews a wink. "Yeah, that would be nice," she said as the two of them got up and left the room.

Kirby and Sue sat alone at the kitchen table. Kirby pulled one last piece of pizza from the pizza tin and put it on his plate. "Wanna share?" He asked Sue.

"No thanks," replied Sue.

"The pizza was good as always." Kirby said and bit into the slice.

"Yeah, I love all of the extra cheese. The pizza shops just can't seem to make it the way I like it."

"Yeah. I know what you mean. Um, so, is everything packed."

"Almost, I still have some small stuff, but I can do that while the movers load the truck tomorrow morning," Sue said.

"I can let you do that if you want to. I don't want to--." Kirby stopped as his eyes began to get glassy. He set his slice of pizza down on his plate and looked across the table at Sue. "Sue, this sucks. I don't want you to go. I feel like I finally found a real friend and now you're being ripped away from me. I'm going to miss you something crazy," he said.

"I'll miss you too," Sue said as her chin began to quiver as she tried to hold back her tears.

Kirby saw that Sue was about to cry. "I promise to email you every day. Maybe we can get web cams and we can talk to each other and see each other every day, kind of…," Kirby said in an effort to cheer her up and keep her from crying.

"Yeah, that would be nice." Sue stood up and walked over to Kirby. He then stood up and wrapped his arms around her. They both walked outside into the backyard and sat on the large swing on the porch. Together they sat with their arms around each other and held hands. They swung back and forth while talking and laughing about the events of the last few weeks and months. They talked about Monika and Janie, about Henry and Myron. Sue joked with Kirby about the goofy hair cut that he used to have. He replied with a joke of his own and told her that he will go back to that style on Monday so that none of the other girls were tempted by his good looks. For a few hours they sat and enjoyed their one last night with each other.

All too soon Sue's dad came out and said that Kirby's mom was waiting for him out in the car.

"Thanks for everything, Mr. Andr -- Ron. Good luck out in California." Kirby said and held his hand out.

"Kirby, you and your Mom will have to come out and visit us once we get settled," Mr. Andrews said as he took Kirby's hand and gave it a firm shake.

"That would be nice. I'd like that," Kirby said.

"Alright, well, you two say good night and don't leave your mom waiting Kirby."

"I won't," He said. "Goodnight, Ron."

As soon as Sue's dad walked back inside Sue wrapped her arms around Kirby and squeezed him as tight as she could. She began to cry and held onto him with all of her might.

Kirby wrapped his arms around her waist and put his head on her shoulder. "It's going to be all right, Sue. I'll never forget you," He said and then kissed her one last time. "Goodnight. I'll miss you!" He whispered in her ear as he turned and slowly walked away.

"I'll miss you--" She said, but he was already gone. "I'll miss you too," she said quietly. Sue began to cry even harder as she sat back down on the large wooden porch swing. The cool night air blanketed her in a calming breeze. Her hair fluttered and flipped in front of her face where it stuck to the tears that were streaming down her face.

Moving Day

Saturday Morning - Moving Day

There were several large men stumbling around the house loading boxes and furniture into the large moving truck that took up most of the street in front of their house.

"Be careful with that box. It contains the good china set," blurted out Aunt Elizabeth to the passing men as they carried boxes out of the house.

"We have good china?" Sue asked.

"Who knew," laughed Mr. Andrews. "Sue, did you check your closets one last time for anything you might have forgotten?"

"Yes, Dad! For the hundredth time I have everything packed up." Sue paced around the front lawn thinking about her new life in California and about leaving Kirby. She kicked at a clump of grass in frustration.

"Well, then I guess that's it. The guys will be finishing up soon. Let me give the driver a little tip and I guess that we can be on our way."

"Okay. I guess." Sue took one last slow walk through the house. She walked into the den where she and Kirby almost had their first kiss. She walked into the kitchen where she had made so many pizzas. She thought about the first time that Kirby had come over to her house and how shy he'd been. He almost hid inside his jacket. She wished that she had that jacket right now to hide in and to take with her to hold and help comfort her whenever she became home sick or missed Kirby. So many memories that she was leaving behind in this house, but there were so many new memories to make in California she tried to tell herself. She walked back out the front door and sat on the front steps.

"Elizabeth, can you please make sure that the doors get locked when the movers are done loading the truck? Ms. Davis, the realtor, will be by in the morning to pick up the keys. Thank you." Mr. Andrews gave Elizabeth a big hug and turned to Sue who was once again standing in the front yard.

"Okay, saddle up, Susie-Q. The wild west is waiting." Ron Andrews took one last look back at the house before he walked over to his car and opened the driver's side door. He sat down, shut the door, and started the engine.

Sue hugged her Aunt Elizabeth goodbye and then took one final look down the street. She half expected to see Kirby riding his bike on his way over to see her off.

"It will be okay, Sue. I'm sure that he'll write and call often," said Aunt Elizabeth. "He's a good kid," she said patting Sue on the shoulder.

"Yeah, I just thought he'd show up." Sue turned and headed off to the car. She took another look down the street before getting into the car and shutting the door.

Mr. Andrews and Sue waved as the car slowly moved forward and pulled away from the house.

Down at the opposite end of the block the city bus came to a stop and let out a handful of passengers. One of them, a young boy, ran from the group of exiting passengers and shouted loudly. "Sue! Sue! Don't go yet!" The boy yelled.

It was Kirby and he was running feverishly down the street. "Sue! No! Don't go yet!" He yelled at the top of his lungs, but he was too late. The Andrews' car reached the far end of the block and turned the corner. He reached the front yard of the Andrews' house. With his jean jacket in one hand he stopped and sat on the grass with his head down.

"She waited as long as she could, Kirby." Aunt Elizabeth stood next to him in the yard.

"I wanted to surprise her and give her this," he said and he held out his jean jacket. "For some reason she loved this stupid thing. The bus got caught in traffic and–and I…" Kirby began to weep softly.

"Kirby, how about we surprise her and we'll put the jacket in the back of the moving truck? This way it will be the first thing that she sees when they open it up in California."

Kirby dried his face on his sleeve and stood up. "That's a great idea."

The Beginning of the Lonely Summer

Sue and her father had taken the long way to California and had stopped along the way to visit what Mr. Andrews had considered to be several of the best offbeat tourist spots known to man. Together they had seen The Jesse James Feather Duster of Death, the World's Third Largest Fire Hydrant, the Smokey Bear Museum, and spent three complete days in Roswell, NM gawking at every UFO related attraction that they could find. When they had finally reached their new home in the sunny Hollywood Hills all of their possessions were already there waiting for them.

Mr. Andrews made a right turn into an opening at the end of a long row of very high hedges. Hidden within the ominous shrubbery was a small circular driveway that lead up to a large off-white house. Two tall columns flanked the mammoth front door. Sue stared at the door in amazement, shock, and anxiety.

"This is all ours now," quipped Ron Andrews. "Are you excited?" he asked of Sue.

"I guess," she replied.

The car came to a stop in just past a water fountain that depicted two chubby cherubs frozen in a playful pose; each with water shooting from their mouth directly at the other. Ron Andrews turned off the car and the tick-tick-ticking of the hot car almost seemed to create a musical medley with the babbling bubbling sound of the fountain. It was soothing and in a weird way began to calm Sue's anxiety.

"Yeah, I guess this is nice," she said.

"Come on, let's get out and take a look around. You're going to love it."

Together Sue and her dad walked along the side of the house, through a vine covered archway, and into the sprawling backyard. The lawn was a rich green color. The sunlight reflected off the big bright blue pool and briefly blinded Sue. She shaded her eyes and it was then that she saw the rock formation that held the twisty water slide. It was everything that she'd ever wanted, and more, but her thoughts kept slipping back to Kirby and how he would have loved to see this. She knew that he'd be making corny jokes and probably would have jumped into the pool with his clothes on. Sue began to laugh; a little chuckle at first, but it quickly grew to a hardy uncontrollable laugh. Sue looked up at her dad and in one quick motion ran full speed directly at the pool and launched herself into the deep end. Ron Andrews laughed, kicked off his sneakers, and followed right behind her.

Thousands of miles away Kirby sat on the curb in front of his house. His bike was upside down and his greasy hands worked the chain of his bike back onto the gears. The sun was hot on his back and he thought about going inside to get some lemonade or at least to enjoy some of the cool refrigerator air. When he had gotten the chain back on he flipped the bike right side up and hopped on the seat. He peddled around in circles in the road. He thought about heading off to the library so that he could check his email, but instead decided to ride to the ice cream stand a couple blocks down the street.

Kirby was moving along pretty fast as he rode his bike into the parking lot at the ice cream stand. He slammed on his brakes and pitched his bike sideways. His tires screeched and kicked up small pebbles from the dirty asphalt. He dropped the kickstand and stepped off his bike. He drove his hand into his front pocket and pulled out a wadded up five dollar bill. As he walked to the front of the building he saw Janie Sinclair sitting on the front steps talking to a couple of other girls that he did not know.

"Hey Janie," Kirby said. He looked down at his grease covered hands and tried the hide them behind his back.

"Hiya Kirby," Janie replied, "these are my friends Lena and Grace."

"Hi," Kirby said.

"Getting' some ice cream?" Janie asked and then rolled her eyes. "Well, I guess you are since you're here." Her friends laughed. "Heard from Sue lately?"

"Not today. Last I knew she was in Roswell trying to get a look at Area 51 or something like that."

"Sounds cool," she said as a car pulled into the lot and the horn honked. "That's my mom. It was good seeing you, Kirby. Give me a call if you get bored this summer and want to hang out."

"Uh, sure," Kirby said. "Nice to meet you Gracie and Lena." Kirby smiled.

The three girls waved as they climbed into the faded blue minivan.

Kirby went into the ice cream stand and ordered a large chocolate and vanilla twist with rainbow sprinkles. After paying for it he went back outside and sat on the front steps. His ice cream began to quickly melt in the summer heat. Just then an old pickup truck with primered doors pulled into the lot. The passenger door opened and out hopped Henry Martin. For a moment Kirby began to panic and almost dropped his cone.

Henry walked closer to where Kirby was seated. His beat up sneakers scrubbed at the parking lot. Kirby could feel melted ice cream as it began to run down his wrist, but did nothing to stop it. He thought about his last encountered with Henry and feared for the worst.

Henry's dad yelled out the open passenger door, "Don't forget to get your momma a lemon ice!" As Henry neared Kirby he turned back to face the truck and nodded. The shadow of Henry Martin, school bully, cast itself over Kirby Carson. By now ice cream ran to and dripped from Kirby's elbow and onto the steps. Henry paused for a moment and looked down at Kirby. "and boy, don't dilly dally. We got a lot of yard work to do," yelled out Henry's dad.

"Alright Pop," he yelled back and then bound up the steps and into the ice cream shop.

Kirby quickly got to his feet, cleaned off his arm with a mound of napkins that was on a nearby picnic table, and headed over to his bike where he finished his ice cream on his bike ride back home.

The California Surprise

Although they were dripping wet Sue and her dad walked into the house in search of towels.

"I think that the linen closet is this way," Ron Andrews said.

Sue followed behind him leaving watery footprints behind her on the tile floors. At the top of the stairs her dad opened a closet door, pulled out some new towels and tossed one at her. "I think your room is over there," he pointed to the door at the end of the hallway. "Go get changed and we'll get something to eat."

Sue began to swipe at her body with the towel as she walked to the end of the hall and opened the door. Before her eyes was a room that was twice the size of the bedroom in her old house. There was a king size bed and a large wooden computer desk. On the desk was a shiny new computer. Her jaw dropped in amazement.

"You like it?" he asked.

"Holy cow! Daddy, this is amazing!" she exclaimed. "Oh my—," her voice trailed off. Sue walked to the foot of her bed. Hanging on the back of her closet door was Kirby's jean jacket. The Led Zepplin back patch had caught her eye first. She rushed over to it and snatched it from the hook. She held that jacket tight to her chest and began to cry. "This is the best surprise ever. Thank you!"

"I, I had nothing to do with it really. Aunt Elizabeth told me that Kirby had stopped by just after we had left and that they put the jacket in the moving truck. She wanted to make sure that I knew it was there so that it wouldn't get lost. Looks like the maid might have ironed it, but I told her not to wash it."

Sue clutched the jacket tighter and tighter.

"Why don't you get dried off and then we can give Kirby a call," he said. "Okay?"

"Sure thing," said Sue. "I'll be right down."

Mr. Andrews shut the door and went to his own bedroom where he changed into some dry clothes.

RING – RING

"I'll get it," yelled out Kirby. "Uh, hello?" he said as he picked up the receiver.

"Hey Kirby!"

"Hey Susie! How ya doin'? Are you okay? Sounds like you're crying?" Kirby began to get nervous that something horrible had happened.

"I'm okay, I'm okay," she said. "I've been crying, but it's all good. We got to the house today and your jacket was there waiting for me. You're the best boyfriend ever," she told him. Kirby was relieved. "You gotta see this house. It's insane," she said.

They talked on the phone for about an hour. Sue told him all about the house, and the pool, and that they had a maid.

"Sue," Kirby said, "I hate to cut this short, but I have to go shower and get to bed. My mom got me a job down at the diner and tomorrow is my first day."

"Yeah, that's cool," Sue replied. "I don't want you to be tired for your big day. I'll write you tonight."

Not that Sue could see it, but Kirby was smiling.

"Kirby?"

"Yeah?"

"I miss you," she said.

"Yeah, I miss you too," he replied. "I miss you a lot."

"If you get a chance go to the library tomorrow and write me back. I want to hear all about your job and everything you've been up to."

"I will. Oh, I almost forgot to tell you. I saw Janie today at the ice cream stand down the street. She said to say hi and even told me to call her if I got bored this summer. And I saw Henry Martin, but nothing happened. I'll tell you all about it tomorrow. Talk to you soon."

"G'night, Kirby."

"Night Susie-Q," Kirby said and then hung up the phone.

Sue sat on the edge of her bed and began thinking again about all of the people back home like Janie and all of her friends from school, and even Henry Martin. She began to get sad, but then remembered Kirby's jacket. She slipped her arms into the sleeves which were too long. The cuffs hung over the end of her fingers. She rolled the sleeves back enough to expose her hands. She then reached up and pulled at the collar; she pulled at both sides until her face was buried and hidden from view.

Sue found comfort and strength in Kirby's jacket. Somehow she knew everything would be okay.

Who Wants To Order Pizza?

Two months had passed. Kirby and Sue had kept their promise of emailing each other every day. Kirby spent most of his free time at the public library engaged in lengthy IM sessions with Sue. They were 2000 miles apart, but with the help of the internet they had done their best to keep the flame of teenage romance alive.

'All right, I'll see you then' Kirby typed and then presses ENTER on the keyboard. With an audible *BING* the message was sent.

"Kirby, I've told you too many times this summer. The library computers are supposed to be for research purposes only. Please tell your mother that I said hello."

"I'm sorry. I'll tell her that you said hello, Ms. Lancaster."

Although Kirby's job at the diner took up a lot of his free time, he had still found plenty of time to get to the library. Plus, since he'd been working he had been saving up to buy his own computer. Kirby logged off the library computer terminal. "I'll be seeing you, Ms. Lancaster. I'm getting my own computer this weekend. I saved up all summer and tonight mom and I are going to go pick it up."

"That's very good, Kirby. A little hard work never hurt anyone. Take care now."

Kirby stood up, gathered up his belongings, and walked out the exit.

The next day Kirby's alarm clock began ringing at six a.m. He got up, dressed quickly and rushed out. He hopped on his bike and peddled away down the road. It was as if Lance Armstrong was powering his bike as he sped through town. After a few miles of riding he was out of breath, but he was finally at his destination; a large two story white house with a white picket fence in front. Planted in the front yard was a FOR SALE sign with a smaller SOLD placard stuck on top of it.

He peddled into the front yard and dropped his bike on the grass. He went and sat on the front steps staring impatiently up and down the street. Finally he saw what he has been looking for; a large maroon Dodge Charger.

He saw the Andrews' car turn the corner and head toward the house. It was the same car that two months prior had taken away his girlfriend and was now delivering her back to him.

Kirby jumped up from the steps and ran down to the driveway to meet them.

Following slowly behind the car is a large moving truck.

As the car pulled into the driveway Kirby ran to the passenger side. When the car came to a stop he quickly opened the door. Sue jumped out, tan and smiling. She tossed his jean jacket at him. "I thought you might want this smelly thing back," she laughed and launched herself into his arms. Mr. Andrews just grinned and shook his head.

"Hey, Kirby," Mr. Andrews said as he exited the car. "Long time no see. What's shakin', buddy?"

"Hi, Ron it's so good to see you guys! Sorry to hear that your recording contract didn't work out." Kirby said.

"Yeah, I guess the world wasn't ready for another round of The Ronster Romp."

"At least you're back here!" Kirby said still holding Sue in his arms.

"Yeah, at least we're back!" Sue agreed. "Let's go inside and check out the new house!"

The three of them went into the house and began to look around. Outside the moving men opened the large rear doors of the truck and looked in at the mountain of boxes and furniture that all needed to be brought into the house.

Inside the house Kirby, Sue, and Mr. Andrews stood in the empty kitchen. "Hey, you guys wanna order a pizza?" Mr. Andrews asked.

THE END

Ryan ONeil was born and raised in Upstate New York, but it was the hustle and bustle of Long Island and the love of a pretty woman that beckoned him to pull up roots and move away from home. His free time is spent with his wife and two extremely energetic children. He is a fanatic baseball fan (GO YANKEES!!!) and has a passion for bacon, barbecued meat, and 80's glam rock.

Facebook: http://www.facebook.com/PlainOldKirbyCarson

Follow Ryan on Twitter: @mrrockdog

Steven Novak (Cover Artwork) - For as long as far as he can remember he has been drawing, writing, and wasting massive amounts of time creating things for no reason other than his own amusement. After honing his talents at the "Columbus College of Art and Design" he moved to California where he was married and began a career as a professional freelance illustrator and writer. He currently lives with his wife Tami, who is not only a primary school teacher, but his muse, best friend, and the only person willing to put up with his terrible jokes and constant need for positive reinforcement.

Novak Illustration: http://novakillustration.com

Follow Steven on Twitter: @stvfoolery

Literary Underground - http://litunderground.com

www.ingramcontent.com/pod-product-compliance
Lightning Source LLC
Chambersburg PA
CBHW071330130626
46556CB00004B/1825